HUNTING WITH DIANA

HUNTING
WITH
DIANA

DAVID
WATMOUGH

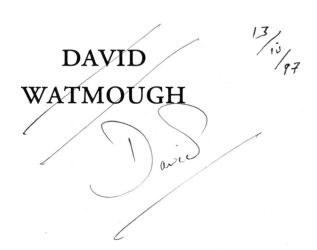

13/iv/97

David

ARSENAL PULP PRESS
VANCOUVER

ARSENAL PULP PRESS
103-1014 Homer Street
vancouver, B.C.
Canada v6b 2w9

The publisher gratefully acknowledges the assistance of the Canada Council
and the Cultural Services Branch, B.C. Ministry of Small Business,
Tourism and Culture.

The author acknowledges the following sources: *The Marriage of Cadmus and
Harmony* (Roberto Calasso); *A History of Greek Literature* (Albrecht Dihle);
The Oxford Companion to Classical Literature (2nd edition) (edited by M.C.
Howatson); *Microsoft Bookshelf '94* (CD-ROM); *Microsoft Encarta* (1994 edition) (CD-ROM); *Early Greek Myth* (Timothy Gantz); *The Greek Myths* (Rob-
ert Graves); *Greek Lyric Vol. 2* (translated by D.A. Campbell); "and to my
friend and earliest tutor in Greek: The Reverend H.W. Last, m.a."

Several of these stories have appeared in slightly different form in the follow-
ing journals and anthologies: *Modern Words, Gayme, The Gay Review,
Dalhousie Review, His* (Faber & Faber), *Queer View Mirror* (Arsenal Pulp
Press), and on the Internet in *Treeline* and *Interbang*.

Printed and bound in Canada by Kromar Printing

CANADIAN CATALOGUING IN PUBLICATION DATA:
Watmough, David, 1926-
  Hunting with Diana

  ISBN 1-55152-032-X
  I. Title.
PS8595.A8H86 1996   C813'.54   C96-910033-7
PR9199.3.W37H86 1996

CONTENTS

To Terri, who shares legends with me,
and Stephan, who taught me to express
them electronically. And also to Diana Filer,
the A *and* Ω *of this particular inspiration.*

"οἱη περ φὺλλῶYη γενγη, τοιη
δε καὶ 'ανδρῶn"

"As the generation of leaves, so is that of man."

—HOMER

And for Thelma e Mike
The author's beloved relatives (cousins)
and friends.

Love XX
David

FOREWORD

In writing this series of fictions I had two major considerations. First, to let the imagination loose after reading a variety of the primarily Greek myths and legends which have been an obsession of recent years. Secondly, to update, refashion and then incorporate these mostly Hellenistic tales of murder, love, cannibalism, warrior bravery, sibling and parental incest, aristocratic courage—and other grossly "politically incorrect" yet atavistic experiences—into the contemporary world of the Internet as I began my own creative odyssey along the electronic highway.

Sometimes my wings are made of fax; sometimes I sail my invisible modem craft through the vast and populous reaches of the Internet. What follows are my adventures into often startling knowledge of those unseen others with strange appetites and arcane disguises.

None of these are truly novel; but all are echoes of the human experience as first encoded and shaped in the glorious imaginations of Classical Greece. Part of my Internet-aroused ambition was to reincarnate these ancient western treasures into the ultimate of contemporary literary fabrics. I wanted to fashion these encounters which I found in the language of Homer and Hesiod and to release them in contemporary images in the newly penetrated spaces of the computer cosmos.

But in writing these, I was not intending to update history, nor was I armored by a scholarly objective. Rather, I was enveloped in the cruel unblinking light of an unexpected self-revelation which these solitary journeys along the information highway readily provided.

I have become, as a result, a changed man; bent by aches and pains from the weight of accumulated years but reverting nevertheless to callow youth when from the ancient Aegean seas, I now range daily in search of a rejuvenating encounter with the last new challenge of this dying century.

Here, then, is my account of an electronic odyssey for all those who have yet to undertake the voyage of some two thousand five hundred years.

—DAVID WATMOUGH

"*Thus the heroes achieved that most yearned for states in which the distinction between lover and beloved begins to blur. Between Orestes and Pylades, it would have been difficult to say which of the two was the lover, since the lover's tenderness found its reflection in the other's face as in a mirror.*"

—ROBERTO CALASSO,
The Marriage of Cadmus and Harmony

FAXES, FRIENDSHIP, AND ARTEMIS

Artemis, deceptively crushed in the vestibule at overheated first-nights at the Vancouver opera, where mink vied with sable on the backs of squat matrons, and stomach-extended men in dinner jackets sweated hastily consumed drinks before entering the darkness to snore their boredom.

Artemis, at the Playhouse, at concerts in the Queen Elizabeth Theatre, where she swirled and twirled about during intermissions, and talked up a sophisticated storm with a glass in one hand and menthol cigarette in the other.

Artemis everywhere.

Perhaps it wasn't how well I knew Artemis but for how long. For in truth we went back. When I first came to the city over thirty years ago I was virtually broke and my prospects were uncertain. No, my prospects were *grim*.

I wanted a job—any kind of job—though in principle I was looking for something with a major newspaper or a prestigious outfit like the Canadian Broadcasting Corporation. My qualifications were slight, to put it mildly. I'd sold newspapers as a schoolboy, and done a couple of radio broadcasts in New York City when I'd first gotten the boat from Southampton. One was a talk on Britain's Angry Young Men (whom I pretended I knew) for WQXR, the *New York Times* station; the other on working in a U.S. Army PX outside Paris that I did for a subscriber station called WBAI. I wasn't paid for either but the experiences had dizzied my expectations and given me lofty aspirations. (And the fact I was only twenty-three at the time might have had something to do with it.)

When I'd first met Artemis she was a receptionist at some rather sleazy downtown office of a now-defunct magazine. I was forlornly ringing doorbells for a job and she took pity on me. In those days it was highly likely you encountered intelligence at the reception desk and ever lower IQs as you climbed the rungs of power in being interviewed from office to office. She was brighter than her editor employer, who wore wire-rimmed eyeglasses, a droopy moustache, and incessantly clicked his nicotine-stained fingers to make a point. He offered a flat no to my job request without even looking up to say it.

Artemis, on the other hand, radiated intelligence as she did a contempt for her balding boss that immediately warmed my heart. "Don't be put off by him," she said, when I'd returned dejected to her front desk. "The man's an idiot! He wouldn't know the difference between Joe Louis and Albert Einstein!"

As for her heart—well, it proved as big as the rare smile that would unexpectedly blossom on her rather severe features. She was a beautiful young woman but it was a classical beauty without hint of softness— until that smile shone forth and momentarily transformed her appearance into warmer, more human constituents.

She would share her lunch sandwiches with me on those days we took the bus down Georgia Street to find a bench at Lost Lagoon and watch the fountains play and the ducks and coots dive and surface, periodically shattering the lake's calm façade. By the time we'd done this a half dozen times I'd gotten a job of sorts—as part-time editorial assistant in a small local publishing house. I liked the copy-editing afternoons, but it paid only peanuts. Their offices happened to be close to hers so it was quite convenient for us to meet.

But it wasn't just sandwiches she gave me. Artemis had a little income of her own, I suspected—for there was no way her job for the finger-snapper could pay for her superior wardrobe, or the pricey restaurants to which she was always referring, or the fistful of dollar bills she'd regularly stuff into my jacket pocket. I never felt I was receiving charity as she quickly drowned my protests with assertions that she'd give it to the nearest panhandler if I didn't shut up. She always said I could pay her back when I got financially on my feet at the press, or landed that job at the CBC I still coveted.

In the end it was Artemis who got the CBC job, as a producer for the *Women's Hour* show, which was awfully popular back in the early 1960s. Shortly thereafter, however, after some six months of knowing me, she abruptly announced she would be leaving Vancouver for Toronto, which was to eventually include both London and Paris.

On her last night she had dinner alone with me in my tiny sixth-floor apartment in the West End. The meal consisted of excessively familiar spaghetti and meatballs, consumed on my card table which I'd draped in a gay linen cloth of Savoyard red squares. We knocked back a bottle of Chianti between us and afterwards said our farewells on the minuscule balcony looking out over the first few highrises then just beginning to sprout around my building, spotting the warm summer's night with pricks of light. Artemis was not to come back, it transpired, for thirty years.

One equally warm June night in 1993 the phone rang. It was Artemis, proclaiming her return to Vancouver. Within a week she was in this house, introduced to my roommate, Ken, and planning a dinner party she abruptly announced she wished to give for us and two men who, like her, had also recently retired to their native city.

That dinner party was instructive. I had suspected before we arrived at the apartment that the men we were to meet were gay. It wasn't a topic that Artemis had ever discussed with me—although from casual references in those early months of our acquaintance, when I had certainly never made a pass at her, I suspected she knew my orientation.

I could not have been in greater error where the other dinner guests were concerned. They were *brimming* with straightness. One was a rather thickset, silvery-haired Italian whom I immediately recognized as a pianist of some renown. The other—whose quick eyes never left the figure of our hostess, and whose lips, I was convinced, correspondingly moistened as his lewd thoughts flew—was an Austrian police official whom Artemis introduced as the onetime head of Interpol.

We were to learn that night that Artemis *only* knew—or at least entertained at her table—straight men of fame, power, or international reputation. Within the first couple of months we had met a Hollywood film star, a High Court judge, the recently retired chairman of World Oil, a former president of the CBC, the owner of the Sizzle and Sear restaurant chain, and Rear-Admiral Olsen of the Royal Norwegian Navy, whom she had met on the ski slopes of Kitsbühl. These men had several things in common: they were all in late middle-age (though the film star went to great cosmetic pains to conceal the fact), all exuded what I can only call a refined lasciviousness, and all were devoted to the person of my old friend.

When I accompanied her on her intensely social rounds—with the description of which I began this memoir—she alluded freely, if sadly, to her various male companions whom I'd met. Sadly, because although she obviously enjoyed them in their several ways, they somehow seemed to fail her in one particular aspect.

Artemis is in my experience an open and frank woman, abrim with acute observation of the human scene to the point her candor can be cutting. But she is not in any sense a coarse person. Her references to sex, for instance, tend to be scintillating and humorous: never crude or four-letter specific. Artemis was and remains a lady in spite of her brilliantly successful career as a woman executive and her general affection and pride in the newly acquired status for her gender. She was also thus very up to date.

Confirmation of that was evidenced on the very first evening we shared her with the pianist and the policeman. In a small room—it was little more than an antechamber, with sparse furnishings and on the wall a simple eighteenth-century engraving of a pair of necking and pecking quails—she kept her personal computer and her fax machine.

As I had just purchased a new, more powerful, version of the former and was contemplating the acquisition of the latter, I questioned her eagerly about both as to their abilities and provenance. I received the impression that while her technical knowledge was not encyclopedic she was quite competent with their use and employed them frequently, "on a daily basis," by her own admission. I was thoroughly impressed by this wholly unknown aspect of my friend and got her to accompany me when I purchased the internal fax modem which she then helped insert in my machine.

It is important to stress here that I had recently joined a local electronic e-mail system and was spending more hours than was good for me engaged in idle chat across the Internet. So for some little time I ignored my new fax and sought to persuade Artemis to join the same group so that we could e-mail each other—a most useful activity, as she was constantly pressing me to accompany her to one event or another.

However, she initially seemed disinclined to involve herself in this further electronic activity. Indeed, she appeared so hectically busy that I perceived her hesitation as born of mere prudence. Once she even snapped at me, exclaiming, "For God's sake stop pressuring me, Davey! I've enough trouble with the stuff I've got, let alone getting involved in a whole lot more."

Now, Artemis and I rarely exchange cross words. In fact, I'd say our relationship was contingent on too much spiritual affinity and shared perceptions for even the slightest vestige of quarreling to manifest itself.

Until the accursed morning, sitting here at this very machine, I had a brainwave—brain attack, I guess I should call it. Artemis and I were going to so many events, exchanging so many dinner parties and lunches (at which I was meeting her seemingly inexhaustible pool of male friends who were constantly flying into town to visit her) that our rendezvous were growing increasingly intricate.

Why not, then, do our exchanges on our dual fax machines? It would not only facilitate all this new social activity, but be a splendid opportunity for me to develop an expertise with what I already perceived as a rather complicated process.

(Usually I would first turn to my partner and ask his advice and opinions. But Ken knew nothing of the computer world and its adjuncts. In fact, he seemed determined to keep things that way and occasionally led me to berating him as a Luddite. He didn't even use an electric typewriter, preferring his old portable Olivetti.)

So the next morning I sent my first message to Artemis. Bearing in mind my neophyte status I made it as simple as possible:

"Hi, Artemis! This is just to say how much I love you and am looking forward to meeting your Anglican Bishop on Monday. Ever, Davey."

I knew she was attending a meeting of the Van Dusen Gardens board of directors that morning, and was being taken to lunch at the Pacific Union Club by the aforementioned Bishop of Leddingham, who was her current houseguest and was also, she had hinted tactfully, an ardent admirer from her London days, so I was not expecting an immediate reply, though I kept my computer on (in whose interior was now the fax), just in case.

I re-sent it that mid-afternoon and again in the early evening, but still I received no response from Artemis. I then pressed a button which intimated it would be sent at regular intervals. As Ken and I were going out that evening, I consequently forgot all about it.

I was reminded forcefully of my faxing debut about three o'clock in the morning. I hadn't replied to two previous phone rings, on the assumption that it was a happy fax message from Artemis which I could read on the morrow. I don't think I would have answered the phone then—except it was the middle of the night and somehow the ringing seemed more insistent, even angrier than usual.

It was well I did so. Otherwise I might well have lost a friend rather than merely suffer the most severe bawling out from her I have experienced to date. An angry Artemis—her voice mercifully subdued because of the proximity of the Bishop in her adjacent bedroom—snarled her ire and frustration.

"Listen, idiot! What the hell do you think you're doing? That bloody fax machine has been rumbling away all night! I told you I was so looking forward to seeing Harry Delos-Browne again and then this happens.

"God, it's been cruel. Dear old Harry—finally, a man I can respond to, who's just the hairy hunk I've been searching for—and I actually manage to get him to forget his cope and miter, to drop his gaiters and crawl into bed.

"We just get in the mood and that bloody fax farts again. Then I have to listen for the second time to the sermon he's giving at Christchurch Cathedral on Sunday before I can remind him of what we were supposed to be doing.

"I had to tug every hair on his chest—he likes that—before he relaxed. He got too relaxed so then I had to apply every technique in the book before he again became the man I knew in the Bishop's Palace in Leddingham back in '75.

"Then what do you think happened next? Of course you know what happened. That goddamned fax started up all over again! He shot from the gorilla position to that of a praying mantis in a split second. That's how I've left him. I expect him to be fast asleep, you creep, when I get back in bed with him.

"Now, Davey, will you please pull that bloody thing out of the wall and *never, never* disturb my precious and rare love life again!"

The phone clicked. I dutifully switched off my errant computer and crept back to our bedroom and trod on the cat as I made my way bedwards in the darkness.

Artemis and I are now reconciled but we do not fax. In fact, it took me several weeks before I got up courage to fax anyone else, and that's only those who are out of town. Now my only failure in the courage department is when it is time to open and digest the fax-inflated phone bill.

MAIDEN VOYAGE

The clue to the whole business was the fact it was not even 6 p.m. I'd say it was about a quarter to the hour. How can I be so sure? Simple. Ken hadn't yet brought us our martinis and ostensibly I was still at work on the book review I was writing for a deadline the next morning.

Truth was, I'd gotten tired of the biography of yet another prickly author who had won this prize and that, yet seemed an inveterate ingrate. Whereas I, Davey Bryant, would have been all smiles and well-wishing if I'd even got a local book award for once in my life. Such is the objectivity one novelist brings to the work of another. . . .

So I played hookey and went back on the Internet. If Ken were to peek through the doorway and announce drinks were on their way, I could quickly return to my word processor and the review article required of me. By the time I heard ice clinking I'd be putting the finishing touches to my dispatch of the biography of the curmudgeonly Aussie, Patrick White, the Nobel Prize winner.

I knew enormous delight as I swiftly and accurately traversed all the specified channels to bring me to discussion on the network. I felt like our old sheep-dog, Mick, back on the farm, wagging his tale when he'd finally gotten all his panicky flock into the safety of the willow-fenced stockade.

A query flashed before me: "How old are you?"

When the question unfolded via its little green letters across the monitor I made a series of assumptions: that the man asking me was younger than me, that he was 'cruising' on the Internet, and that he'd been burned in the past by ending up wasting his time with some wrinkled ancient. A cautious man, I decided, yet not one inclined to beat about the bush.

I thought of responding with: "Older than you but younger than you think." Instead, I ignored the question and asked him what his interests were and whether he was involved professionally in the geriatric health business.

"I'm interested in the ecological movement. Are you worried about all the trees being destroyed here in British Columbia?"

I said yes but that I was for saving humans, too.

My electronic correspondent paused. I took the opportunity to expatiate further. "I am an enemy of simplistic solutions to everything. People are so solipsistic in their concerns—especially the crusaders."

The response wasn't what I expected. "You must be quite old. Also, I don't know what solipsistic means."

"Sorry about that. How about egotistical assholes instead?"

That seemed to reassure him. "I don't like creeps like that either. But I don't like big words as well."

My fingers skimmed the keys—blessed for once without typos as I mounted my favorite hobby-horse. "Then we are in even further agreement. I loathe all the jargon that passes for profundity these days. I believe short words are much more useful than those pompous ones with a pseudo-scientific basis. Give me blind, deaf and crippled—to sightless, aurally-impaired, and physically handicapped!"

I warmed to my harangue. "Not to mention the parts of the body—who needs testicles, urine and excreta when we have balls, piss and shit?"

I paused. I'd not only run out of steam but realized suddenly I was breaking the rules. That Internet choreography obliged me to share the writing time equally when there were just two people chatting.

Out of the upper space on my screen he responded: "How old did you say you were?"

"You seem unhealthily interested in age," I answered testily. "Do you have a problem with your own? Something psychological?"

Of course behind my irritation lurked a degree of fear. I am usually not all that vain about my age but somehow in the bleakness of the Internet I was loathe to chalk up the bleak figures of six-o. Especially to be mocked or patronized by callow youth.

I need not have worried.

"My name is Kypria and I am thirteen. Please don't get grumpy. I like talking to you. You don't use too many words I don't understand. Not like Daddy does. He sure would be angry if he knew his little girl was sitting here using his PC."

It was my turn to be slow in reply. I recalled some of the lewd thoughts that had been flirting around the fore of my mind up to that point. I sweated. Jesus! Thank God she had finally put a sex and an age to these little landmines that flowed so facilely across my screen.

At least that also meant she couldn't see my blush: the anonymity worked both ways.

I drew a deep breath. "I didn't think you could be too old. You don't use jargon yet and you certainly aren't pompous. I'm sure your Daddy is proud of you being able to enter the Internet. I'm certainly impressed."

Perhaps I started right then being wise after the event but from then on in her extreme youth seemed to shape and illumine her words.

"What do you think of Jesus?"

I thought very carefully. "I think he was very nice. Why? Don't you?"

"Are you a Christian?"

Visions of the fanatics of the Christian Right and their hate-filled attitudes jumped into my mind, even if such images sat ill with the computer literate youngster with whom I was conversing.

For years I have resolutely refrained from argument with those simplistic bigots who think God comes exclusively to them on specific bits of paper adorned with the stately prose of sixteenth-century English. I certainly wasn't going to debate with the progeny of such people.

"In a way," I typed diplomatically. "But 'Christian' is a very broad term nowadays, don't you think?"

"What do you think of Charles Darwin?" she replied unexpectedly.

It occurred to me that Miss Kypria was a young lady not disposed to linger over topics where my response was less than satisfactory. But whether she was youthful or not, I wasn't about to surrender all caution.

"My grandfather knew the Huxleys," I told her. "They were great friends of Darwin. I've kept up vaguely with the later generation of Huxleys—at least I did when I was still a student." I paused for a moment. "That was some time ago, of course."

That didn't give her mere pause; it shut her up. In fact, for a moment there I thought she'd fled. When she did reply it was from distinctly left field.

"Are you an environ—a green?"

That was easier, I felt. "Yes, I am. We have to properly rethink our whole attitude to the environment."

She returned to an earlier topic. "Where do you stand on Clayoquot Sound?" she asked, referring specifically to a disputed area on Vancouver Island over which environmentalists and logging interests were currently ranged in violent dispute.

I decided to play the devil's advocate. "For saving the trees of course," I wrote, "provided we don't put anyone out of work. I love trees but I like children to have food and clothing and grow up in a community, too, don't you? People have roots as well as trees, you know."

I was not to learn whether she did or not. "Do you have a wife?"

Of course she couldn't see the old caution flit across my face. "Why do you ask?" (Thank God a tremble in the voice goes unrecorded on the Internet.)

"I wanted to know whether you let her use your computer? Daddy is very selfish with his."

"I have a partner. And he's a 'he.' He doesn't know much about this computer stuff. Nor is he all that interested."

"He's like my Mom, then."

I let that one go.

"I shall have to start helping him get dinner ready soon," I lied. "We're having poached salmon—a whole sockeye—and it takes a while in the steamer."

Her reply was speedy. "I'm a vegetarian. I don't eat fish or meat."

I couldn't be sure whether she was being smug or not but the mere words were angular enough to irritate.

"Quite right," I typed. "At your age vegetables are far more import-ant. Plenty of spinach and broccoli. Lots of pasta, eh?"

"Now you are being old with me, which I don't like."

I thought she was through and I was about to offer something a little more placatory when she started right up again.

"I believe in abortion as well as for keeping Vancouver a nuclear-free city. And I think pot should be legalized—though Mr. Cameron, our school principal, doesn't."

"Then he's part of the straight establishment," I finally felt free to reply. "Well thank God, Kyria, neither of us are part of that!"

"Kypria," she corrected. "Yes, I'm glad too. Hey, I've got to go now. I can hear my Dad in the driveway. Nice talking to you on the Internet."

And she was gone. I sat there a while, baffled. I'd wanted to ask her more questions. I had no quarrel with her pert pat answers to so many things. But I wanted to embarrass her, wanted to ask her awkward questions like whether she had started her periods yet, and whether she had a boyfriend and if so what did they get up to. But now she was not only gone but most likely vanished from my screen forever. Possibly— no, probably—the last time I'd talk to an unknown little girl of thirteen for the rest of my gay existence. Then that's the way of the Internet. Ships that pass . . . that kind of thing.

Another thought occurred to me as I turned on my swivel chair to greet my lover, extending a tray of hors d'oeuvres and two filled glasses. I was glad I hadn't asked her those last questions. Relieved. It was as if I'd been tempted but hadn't let the Internet down. At least, not that time.

COOL CATS

I should have been in bed; if not in the Land of Nod, then desperately trying to get the Sandman to escort me there. Instead I was sitting in the gloom of my study, the only light emanating from the monitor and a few pinpricks along the wainscot informing me the electronic gadgetry was alive and well.

I guess forty, fifty years earlier, when I was also inclined to roam dark rooms instead of placing curls on a cool pillow, my mother would have described me to Daddy as "overstimulated," offered me hot cocoa and insisted I clutch my teddy bear which she'd picked up from the floor, before toddling back to the gabled back room of the creaky old farmhouse where a night-light burned.

Now I'd be more likely described as a crazy old insomniac who was wont to use a belated love affair with the Internet as an excuse for not lying there in the dark, imagining new illnesses in my gut, and worrying about bank accounts and whether we could afford to purchase another of those IRAS (or was it RRSPS?) one's friends confusingly talked about around tax time.

Give me the quiet hum of my steed as I set out on press-button paths to meet unknown people in far places. I'd done it before, of course. Talked in the middle of the night to a presumably drawling Texan whose Daddy had an oil pump in his backyard, to a fellow Vancouverite who wanted me to join his campaign to abolish whale-watching off the west coast of Vancouver Island because he insisted it upset the pregnant ones heading down to Baja California on their annual trek to the Great Gray nursery.

But on this night, as I feverishly scanned the screen for words from an unseen intelligence, I sensed a difference, an excitement that trembled my fingers and for once I knew it had nothing to do with ague or arthritis. I'd call it premonition—if only old-fashioned things like that and esp and hunches and hair-raising all seem somehow so remote from this fleshless and scientifically accurate apparatus at my withered fingertips.

Whatever it was, it happened. And pretty soon after I'd entered the Internet. His name was Gene and he was on-line in Gainsville, Florida. His words seemed to stream across my screen more quickly than mine did. He made fewer spelling mistakes, too. But his sentences were very simple and his language plain.

I soon got the impression that he was an old hand which correspond-ingly made me think he was young. After all, most of the practitioners I've come across seem to be under thirty. (In any case, I am usually on pretty safe ground in concluding that they're a hell of a lot younger than I am.) Gene didn't shilly-shally in this area any more than he did in revealing other personal matters.

"I'm being taken to Miami for my birthday next week as I've gotten some time off from the lab. Do you ever get there? I guess it's an awful long way from the west coast."

I told him I did occasionally visit friends in Baltimore but had never been further south. Then I asked him what kind of lab he worked in—adding that I was a writer-broadcaster who sometimes did semi-popular scientific stuff for magazines when commissioned. I didn't mention I was now retired.

He obviously liked my rather oblique approach to yielding informa-tion, only feeding autobiographical details along with questions asked.

At first, that is. Then things changed. Subtly.

"Do you like sculpture?" he asked. And then, before I had time to unscramble hasty and hazy thoughts about Rodin, Henry Moore, or Michelangelo, he continued: "Know anything about body-sculpture?"

It was the sudden pause before his last spate of written words which quickened my pulse. However, I kept my cool. Procrastinated.

"Like Michelangelo's David?"

"I was thinking of something more personal," I responded. I suddenly thought of a crowded shelf in our living room. "I have a rather nice terra-cotta figure of a nude boy kneeling with a dove on his knees. We got it when we were visiting Gerona in Spain."

I was about to type that the "we" included my lover, Ken, but decided to postpone it until I got at least some clues about Gene himself. I didn't have to wait long. There was a hint already in his sentences that suggested he was about to convey something revelatory to reward my distinctly uncharacteristic patience.

"I was thinking more of warm flesh than cold clay—if you get my meaning."

"You mean like—like pierced earrings?" I typed quickly.

"Something like that. For starters that is. Now just let your imagination wander a bit . . . down from the ears . . . much further down. . . . "

I may have been a bit slow initially at getting his drift. No longer. My imagination was already meandering the erogenous zones of the human body, specifically, a man's body.

My fingers sped. "We still talking rings?"

If it was possible to be coy on a monitor, that was what he now became.

"In a manner of speaking. But not just rings. Sculpture. I have someone who just loves body-sculpture. I have it done for him. He likes to see it on my body. He uses it too."

I didn't want to interrupt but couldn't help racing fingers over the keyboard. "You do the sculpturing, then? The actual carving?"

He wrote back instantly. Dismissively. "Of course not. I get it done. I know a guy at the local hospital. He's into the same scene. Very skilled—can do even the most delicate operation."

"A doctor?"

"Kind of," he wrote cautiously.

I drew a very long breath indeed. "And what precisely does he do?"

"I have a neat stomach ring—22-carat with a ruby in it. Leonard is ape for rubies. It's his birthstone."

I made no immediate contribution to the monitor but that didn't seem to matter. He needed no urging of any kind.

"Next week I'm going to get a special job for my friend's birthday," he wrote. "It's going to involve some piercing as well as some sewing. Real complicated. My friend at the hospital says it will be his most ambitious project to date. Leonard will love it. It means we can do things we've never done before. Things he can do with me when I'm totally in his power. I'm quite excited. You can imagine."

"I'm trying," I wrote, reluctantly joining my green letters to his on the dark screen again. "But what exactly is—involved?"

Gene's words fairly jumped, though that could well have been nervous anticipation of the prospect before him, rather than an attempt at speed writing. "It's really rather complicated, Davey. Like, hard to describe on this screen? Just let me say that Leonard loves to experiment and we are both really into the body sculpture scene. Anything that makes my man happy is okay by me. Get the picture? He's the guy in charge. Do you have a master, too?"

I thought of my probably sleeping lover whose threshold of pain was, if anything, even lower than mine, and typed my response with infinite care.

"Our scene here in Vancouver is a little different. But we're broad-minded. Always willing to learn, as it were." Then I tried to lighten the whole matter. "Apart from sculpture, do you go much in to visuals? I was thinking of tattoos. I guess you could come up with some pretty hot

S&M scenes. Then I suppose there'd always be the danger of being arrested for pornography while sun-bathing or even walking along the beach!"

The top of my screen remained blank for an awfully long time. I bit my lip for surrendering to flippancy and breathed heavy relief when his words finally started to emerge again.

Only there was nothing of body sculpture; not a whiff of sexual role-playing between "master" and "slave." Instead it was cats.

"Do you have a cat? We have both Abyssinians and Burmese."

Staring at me through the dim light of my study, lit only by the monitor screen, was our cat, Wystan—a five-year-old tabby refugee from the local SPCA who had quite erroneous ideas as to his social station and lineage. But Wystan was a loyal friend as well as being a great mouser, and self-appointed custodian of two irrepressible dogs. I was not about to hurt his highly vulnerable feelings.

"Yes, we have a domestic short-hair. His name is Wystan because his purr is distinctly poetic and erudite—like that of Wystan Auden."

I made up the part about the purring even as I stabbed out the words: "We called him Wystan because the day we got him was the anniversary of the poet's death."

But I need not have minded. Gene wasn't really interested in Wystan's pedigree. By now I was beginning to suspect he wasn't particularly interested in mine either.

"Doesn't the surgery hurt?" I asked. "I think I'd faint."

"We are actually thinking of mating one of our Abyssinians, Pharaoh, to our little Burmese miss, Deborah. I think the result would be very exciting. The two breeds are so complementary, we both think."

I can be stubborn. "Some of those parts of the body are so tender. Like the most tender of all, I should think. And what about the chances of infection? These days you can't be too careful, can you?"

"We shall be going to the St. Petersburg cat show this fall. There are rumors of a Burmese-Abyssinian cross going to be presented. Wonder if they'll call it a Burmabby or maybe an Abbyburm. Cute, eh?"

"Is it anything like the Danish operation that Christine Jorgensen went to Denmark for—back in the fifties or sixties, wasn't it?"

"I wasn't born back then." At least that got him off cats. "Anyway, old fella, you know your trouble? You ask too many fucking questions."

My screen went dormant. The wind was certainly out of my sails and he was patently pissed off. I sat there for long minutes before leaving the Internet and, softly summoning Wystan, headed for bed and my coeval lover.

ON THE ROAD TO
CALLUM BAY

There was an irony right from the start. I knew that Ken thought I was spending far too much time on this computer, conversing with and eavesdropping on others using the Internet. So when he artfully proposed we visit Victoria and see one of his numerous grad students who was now on faculty at the university and whom he knew was a particular favorite of mine, I wasn't altogether surprised.

Not that I really needed any persuasion. I always enjoyed trips to the provincial capital. Besides, Wally Moy, now a rising star in Comp Lit, had recently taken up with a young lawyer named Dennis Kennilsworth, and they and we both were anxious for us to see their recently rented home overlooking Ross Bay and the Juan de Fuca Straits, which separates the southern tip of Vancouver Island from the northern end of the Olympic Peninsula in western Washington.

I mention all the geography because that was what we were in fact treated to by the previously unknown Dennis, who proved from the outset to be a likable if slightly pedantic and talkative young man—and thus in sharp contrast to the reserved Wally, a fourth-generation Chinese whose affluent parents still lived in the Kerrisdale home where he'd been born twenty-seven years earlier.

There was something faintly civil-servantish about Dennis even though he, too, was still in his twenties—and quite comely at that.

He also told me—and here came that irony—both he and Wally were ardent computer buffs and frequent travellers of the information highway. In fact, we had not been very long inspecting their pleasant white-frame home before they were both explaining their PC's and the rival claims of Dennis's Word versus Wally's WordPerfect, and that they were both vaguely anti-Apple.

It was at this juncture my roommate left us, wandering back out through the French windows to the Japanese garden that their lazy landlord had installed to eschew the efforts of regularly mowing a lawn. The three of us at once fell to discussing computers, modems and our experiences on the Internet. But my contribution was less than it might have been for I had caught my lover's frowning look when it had dawned on him that he had dragged me away from Vancouver and the claims of my monitor, only to bring me face to face with another one in the home of one of his favorite grad students.

During dinner, over which the boys had obviously exerted themselves in planning (Dennis) and cooking (Wally), the phone rang. We were informed it was a couple who were great friends of theirs, inviting all four of us to their home just beyond the city limits.

Ken's spirits had noticeably soared soon after the computer chit-chat by being served a schooner of Tio Pepe sherry which Wally had flatteringly remembered was a favorite of his old teacher's, and been thoroughly confirmed by the judicious mix of Chinese and French cuisine which the young men had lavished upon us. There was no more arcane electronic talk to deject him and although I suspected that, like me, he would have preferred to stay put after dinner, down a few scotches and enjoy the company of our hosts who were still so evidently in love, he readily agreed to get into Wally's BMW with the rest of us and drive the five miles or so to their friends' residence which we were told was situated dramatically on a windswept headland.

It hadn't been until we were on the way that Dennis had explained that Gerry and Mary Sedgewick, whom we were to shortly meet, were the parents of two children in their teens. As the four of us tumbled out before the gray-weathered house with its heavily moss-covered shake roof I felt fleetingly self-conscious, and glanced quickly at Ken to see if I could read something similar in his expression. After all, we were four men and, as if to give the fact extra emphasis, Ken and I were at least twenty years older than the other two.

Both young men stressed how "gay positive" their friends were. Mary was apparently a lawyer working in the same office as Dennis—his boss, in fact—but they had fast become friends. Her husband, Gerry, a farmer's son like myself, was born on the prairies and, from a social-worker beginning, had become a government consultant.

Mary, tall, small-breasted with a magpie streak of white a startling presence in her swart hair, wore a long denim skirt and affected west coast Native jewelry, earrings with owl emblems etched on dull silver, beads of amber and two prominent rings with Haida-inspired orcas and salmon as their insignia. Her skin was brown from exposure to sun and wind, for she was an inveterate vegetable gardener who devoted long hours of her leisure to the arable plot that was protected from the prevailing winds by the house. All in all there was something hippyish to her appearance: the kind of woman I recalled wandering up and down Vancouver's Fourth Avenue in the counter-culture garb of the late 1960s and early '70s.

Gerry couldn't have presented a more diametrically opposed appearance: he was slightly shorter than his wife with thinning red-gold hair and a pale skin. He had obviously divested himself of his office clothes—to the extent of wearing a plaid shirt and jeans. But his socks were still city-dark and thrust into expensive Florsheim shoes that looked distinctly incongruous out there on the stone-flecked terrain.

They greeted us with unalloyed eagerness and I was at once reassured to see them warmly hug our young friends. We stood there talking at the back of the house facing the open ocean which we could hear sibilantly brushing a beach hidden by clumps of spike bentgrass which was the border to their rude backyard.

The Sedgewicks then led us into a spacious living room with a long, plate-glass window looking out on the scene we'd just vacated, and we sat in comfortable leather armchairs where our drink orders were taken. It was all so very civilized I felt I'd entered some variant version of a *Better Homes & Gardens* magazine world where inside all was comfort but outside raw nature had been allowed to prevail.

That impression, however, was quite devastatingly shattered by the advent of an apparition at the entrance of the living room. Where there had only been a darkening doorway as the evening shadows thickened, there now stood—or, rather, hung over in a curiously stiff fashion—a white-faced youth as gaunt as he was bent. His shoulders were grotesquely stooped, whether from an overall physical affliction or from supporting the ungainly contraption at his side, I was unsure. The reedy voice was sadly congruous with the twisted body, the corpse-like pallor and the insistent clack-clack of the machine with which he was encumbered and which he clutched so tightly with those meagerly fleshed hands.

The sense of the grotesque that had suddenly overwhelmed us was not diminished by Mary Sedgewick addressing the newcomer as if he were the epitome of the ordinary. "Hi, Cliff. These are two pals of Dennis and Wally who've come over with them for a drink and chat." She turned to us, smiling. "This is my son, Cliff. Would you like to show them your room, Cliff? Before they settle down, that is?"

There came some kind of a noise from the boy. I couldn't be sure whether it was a yes or no. Wally obviously took it for the former.

"That's nice, Cliff. You know, we haven't seen your new set-up either. But your Mom has sure told us all about it."

I wondered what in hell Wally was talking about but didn't have to wait too long to find out. No longer than it took Cliff to deftly manipulate his support machinery back through the squeeze of the doorway, and into the room opposite which was obviously his own. There was a mechanically-operated wheelchair at the foot of a rumpled bed, and on the surrounding walls were posters of athletes, college pennants, and other adolescent insignia which in the doleful context wrenched at the heart. There was a blown-up portrait of James Dean, for example, which my sight fled past lest I caught the young man's attention with an unbidden sob or sigh.

I needn't have worried. Cliff's attention, along with that of Wally and Dennis, was already fixated on the long table range of computer equipment that took up two-thirds of the space of his French windows, which also led onto the garden like those of the adjacent living room.

"Of course Cliff had the 486 DX-33 with 8 meg of RAM and all that when you were here last time," his father explained. "But I don't think he had the internal modem, did he?"

Mary continued in like fashion in lieu of any intelligible response from Cliff who, in any case, was preoccupied with getting himself and his contraption to the computer chair. "It's been quite remarkable how quickly he mastered even that," she went on. "It's been less than a month and he's gotten it down pat. He spends hours here. It's been a godsend, hasn't it, Gerry?"

Cliff finally spoke. His voice was still husky and low. But I guess I'd gotten used to it very quickly, for what he had to say made total sense. "I sure like the Internet. After the car crash I stopped going out much." He looked down at himself and at his support device, then smiled so disarmingly that I felt my heart melt. "You can see why, of course. This way I get to know lots of people. You guys use the Internet? It's great what you can do."

My voice trembled with relief when I replied. "Sure is, Cliff. I talk to lots of people. Ask Ken." (For once I didn't mind involving him.)

"He can say that again," Ken said. But he was grinning. My faith was well placed.

The young man slowly turned his large and really quite handsome head. His dry lips were upturned at the edges. I knew that he was enjoying himself, and I felt deep shame at my stupid reactions. "You want to see something?" he asked.

Four gays chorused "yes" in unison. But mother Mary for the first time betrayed just a hint of what seemed like irritation. "That's why they've come to your den, darling. It's why we asked them over." Her voice was calm, but I sensed the darkness behind it.

He turned back to the screen and his bony fingers rattled across the keyboard. I couldn't help it, in spite of the self-reproach. I thought of skeletons. The clicks from his computer now filled the hushed room. Words flew up on the screen—quick, lively words—soon interspersed by others from afar. More intense clicking, and a further flurry of response.

Once more he turned around to the six of us, assembled as a horseshoe around his computer helm staring intensely beyond him, trying to read the screen.

"Don't—don't look at me. Look out of the window." His voice reminded me of his mother's a few moments ago.

We did immediately what we were told. He might be bent under the weight of his damaged body, but there was no doubt now as to who was reigning in that room stuffed with insignia proclaiming handsome flesh and youthful health.

At first nothing happened. There was just the hesitant presence of the Pacific, a greyish distinction from a paler, cloudless sky above. Beyond that the dark smudge of the further coast of the Olympic Peninsula. Then, the miracle. First one pinprick of light. Then another. Winking, flashing.

"That's Port Angeles," murmured Mary. "And further west . . . the road to Clallam Bay."

But her remarks went unheeded as the vision unfurled. As the lights of America grew in number, spread their necklace, it was as if the stars of heaven had come down and embraced the land.

Then a voice now wholly free of tremble or hesitancy—a young, strong voice—spoke.

"They're my friends on the network. And friends of theirs I've never seen. We been working on this. Jeez, I didn't know they were so many. It's neat, huh? Isn't that something, folks?"

You know the cliché about not believing your eyes? Well, this was that, and more. More lights, that is. Not a Milky Way, perhaps; not even the electric rash of a city. But enough bulbs switched on to do a crippled boy's heart good—if the way he was grinning told anything.

As the skinny hands behind us sped their way as if over an organ console, to summon and to thank the pinpricks far across the water, I saw Wally's dark Chinese eyes moisten. Cliff's dad mumbled something about having to use the bathroom. In the semi-dark of the boy's room, Ken's hand went out to brush my adjacent one. Looking up at the sky outside, it seemed to me that even the stars were glowing ever more brighter.

THE DIRTY SECRETS
OF DIOMEDES

No one has a face on the Internet. It is not a place of icons. There are many rocks under which to hide from harsh truth via the shelter of words. Not surprisingly, then, it is a place of refuge for those who shy away from the glare of the candid while paradoxically aching for contact through an impersonal screen.

These were the kinds of reflections that arose during the night I logged on and found myself in conversation with Diomedes Starchos. He told me he was the only son of Greek immigrants, had been raised in Bar Harbor, Maine, and now belonged to a chat group in Montpelier, Vermont.

I've never been quite sure of those details, as we first made contact over a year ago, when my knowledge of the system was scant indeed. All too often, just as I was about to lay hold of some salient information about a correspondent, I was frustrated in mid-sentence by hitting some wrong button so that the monitor either went sky-blue blank or was filled with jittery "hieroglyphics" that kept multiplying their gibberish line after line.

Such a mishap did not happen with Diomedes, though in retrospect there were times when I was tempted to wish it would. Not at first, though. At the start all went swimmingly, as they say. Though perhaps "swimmingly" isn't altogether apt, as one of the first things he told me was that he had recently been involved in a boating incident in which he had nearly drowned while attending summer school at Harvard.

That was by preface to his informing me how he had been profoundly lonely in the local hospital where he had been incarcerated for several weeks with a lung infection he had contracted. On his return to Montpelier he had still felt far from well, and on being told by his doctor that he should take it very easy and stay home as much as possible, he quickly acquired a modem for his computer and thus made acquaintance with the Internet.

It seemed that since then he had not only become a regular on the electronic highway but was now very fussy over whom he would converse with. For instance, mine was the sixth chat he had started that early April morning in 1993.

"I find so many of them boring. They start off as if they've got something to say but they soon show they're only interested in their petty little world. But I hope you're different. I've never talked to a Canadian before."

"I hope I am, too," I stabbed firmly across the screen, "but these computer encounters are always risky. It's a chance you just have to take. After all, you can always switch off. It's a hell of a lot easier than walking away from a bore in a bar, for instance."

My reference to risk seemed to please him. "There's lots of risks in life, aren't there? I've always liked to take risks." There was a slight pause. "It was real rough out there on the Charles River. Dolon didn't want us to go rowing that morning. Then he never liked to take risks."

When he paused again I just waited for him to continue. I dislike probing, though I certainly like to lay hold of the information such digging can yield. You can learn the wildest things.

Patience paid off. "You alone?"

"There's not really room for two at the computer."

"I mean, live alone."

My mental traffic light switched from green to amber. Scavenging for info for my writing purposes was one thing; giving it out was quite another ball game. "Not altogether. My roommate is away quite a lot. On the road. He travels for a pharmaceutical company". My light jumped to red. That was definitely all I was providing from that particular neck of the woods. "You alone, too, then?"

"Yes, sir. I'm alone. Got to cross a bean field and pass a pond before there's anyone else. Human-wise, that is. Got a great dog. Argo is a real companion. It'd be pretty lonesome around here these days without him."

I sensed unspoken themes behind the words. It's the kind of thing—a sixth sense?—that grows on you after a while when you use the Internet. Problem: how to get him to spill what he wanted to and yet not trespass on his space? Sure, it's true I cherish the data of human experience—a scavenger, maybe—but I'm not interested in spiritual larceny. I have no wish to subtly thieve those things he was disinclined to give away.

Unfortunately he saw it otherwise. Or saw me rather differently than I perceived myself.

"You like asking questions more than answering them, right?"

My pulse quickened. I wasn't used to such directness. "It ain't necessarily so—as the old song has it." Then I decided to move in to attack, albeit cautiously. I didn't want to lose my Greek correspondent at this stage. Instinct told me he had more—much more—to offer.

"Perhaps you want to talk tonight more than I do. I'm a bit pooped. I'm also a good listener, my friends tell me."

"So what do you do for a living?"

"I'm a writer. Freelancer, that is. I write fiction, the odd documentary for TV or radio. But I range wider than that. What tired me today was finishing an article on the waning of the sockeye salmon run in the mouth of the Fraser River. I also do some part-time stuff for the university's extension department. Writers in British Columbia aren't exactly fat cats. They have to wear several caps—like most places, I guess."

I stopped. That was enough for him at the moment. Besides, it certainly took care of a lot of accusations that I was all questions and no answers.

"So you're a writer. What you write about?"

A series of importunate questioners at public readings had readied me for that one. "Sex, psychology and outlandish incident. Family life, that is."

It took him a few seconds to digest that.

I ducked in with a question of my own. "Do you read a lot yourself?"

"Not much any more. Used to, though, when I had the time. Even poetry! Now I'm a grad student. Economics. All I can manage is the odd whodunit when I get the chance. Do you write them? Like detective novels? P.D. James?"

I shook my head—and grinned with the realization that there was no one there to see me do so. "Not a hint of gore. Although I do try other ways to express contemporary violence."

"Violence? What kind of violence do you have up there in Canada?" My mind flickered at his repetitious intensity.

"The usual," I wrote. "Why? Is there some kind of specialty in Vermont?"

But Diomedes was apparently in no mood for humor. "How do you people execute your killers? The chair? Or is it still hanging? Or injection like some of the States?"

"We don't have capital punishment anymore in Canada."

"You don't? You get a lot of murders, then?"

"Not especially. There's no connection between the two, you know."

Something was bothering me. Nothing Diomedes had written on the screen suggested he was some kind of right-wing freak—into the NRA or various forms of revolting state execution. Yet he certainly didn't want to let the matter drop.

"I guess you get a lot of guys fleeing U.S. justice in Vancouver? That must be a problem."

I was getting a *little* tired of this route. "I really wouldn't know. As I said, I'm a freelance writer, not a police official. By the way, I think there is some chat group on the Internet that deals with justice and prisons."

"I'm just getting your opinion. You seem real cool about these things. I am very interested in your answers. We don't hear about these things from Canadians. Only about socialized medicine and the weather you send down to us."

I could have pointed out that I'd told him nothing—not really answered his initial question about violence. But I decided it would be a waste of time. Diomedes didn't appear to be the type who was easily deflected. Equally, I could have terminated the conversation, but my interest in him and his motives had certainly not flagged. To the contrary, I was more intrigued than ever with whatever it was that seemed to lurk behind his words.

"Fairly safe where you are there in Montpelier, I should think."

"Sure. Like I said, here on the outskirts of town there's just that pond and a beanfield—and beyond that the local cop shop." He then typed the ha-ha sign of ":-)".

"And I told you about my dog, Argo. He's a Rottweiler. Bit of a killer when he was a puppy. A few sheep, someone's dachshund, and a toy poodle. And there was talk of him doing in my neighbor's cat. But she hates Greeks and is always causing trouble for me. Anyways, Argo has quieted down a whole lot. Boston is a way different from here, I can tell you that. You heard of the Boston Strangler? I used to pass his house on my way to the subway each day. Sort of creepy."

"There's very little strangling here. The weather isn't conducive. Not enough humidity in the summer. Strangling thrives more on hot and sticky nights. Passions run higher then, don't you agree?"

I thought my ruse to get him to shift his direction had worked.

"Boston is the pits for weather. In the winter you freeze your balls off and in the summer you fry them. Then there are those times when the wind blows in off the Atlantic. There are people I know who get real disturbed. Like my gramps used to say happened all the time in the Mediterranean. Those north winds he called the Boreas when he was back in the old country."

I encouraged him. "Yes, indeed. I've heard the same thing about the Mistral in southern France. Does the weather affect you?"

The response came swift as a bullet. "No. Never."

I darted away. "Personally, I can't stand eastern humidity. My partner and I fled New Jersey because of it. That's how we ended up in Vancouver."

"What's your take on drowning?" This comment was unexpected.

Again I thought a frivolous route was the best to take. "I'm against it. How about you?"

"I got a theory. We all came from the water in the first place and that's where, deep down, we all want to end up. If there's a heaven I figure it's watery."

His words were coming up on the screen much more slowly, almost as slow as mine. But mine were governed by ineptitude. In another, *pre-mouse* era, I had been a hunt-and-peck typist. The pauses were so marked, so frequent, I could easily have inserted my comment. But his tortuous articulation precluded any such thing.

"When we left the boathouse you couldn't tell what the Charles was like. There was a breeze, for sure, but when isn't there one over water? But around the bluff I guessed what it was going to be like. In fact I knew we could easily be in trouble. It's not easy battling waves in a skiff.

"From the stern, I put one hand over the gunwale end down into the water. Dolon rowed like mad amidships to keep us midstream. The river was brown—muddy, I guess, from being churned up by the wind. And God, it was cold! That water was colder than a witch's tit! We aren't talking about winter, either. I'd seen the ice break-up coming downriver a good month earlier. There were already buds on the goddamned forsythia. And all the dirty little piles of dog-shit speckled snow on the sidewalks had gone.

"I'd joined him rowing, picked up the rhythm when I noticed something funny. There was no one else out there on the river. Remember, I'm not talking stormy weather. Looking up, the sky was a beautiful blue. You got to be there in New England in late spring to get a blue like that. There were a few clouds around, little fluffy things, only they were whiter than goddamned white where the sun lit them up.

" I tell you, when you looked up you wanted to think clean things, take your mind away from that dark water swirling harder and harder, and smacking against our prow and drenching Dolon with spray until he was gleaming wet.

"I've fooled around in boats all my life. As a tiny kid my Dad took me out off Bar Harbor. Jesus! The Atlantic can be real shitty there. But there was nothing to prepare us for what happened. I know Dolon was as surprised as me. I swear we didn't hit anything, no object under water or anything like that. One moment we were paddling like mad and bouncing like a top against heavy waters. The wind was strong enough for us to have to holler to hear each other. I had to scream and yell to suggest we move further over to port where there was more lee than out there in the middle of the Charles. We'd taken in a little water but nothing to make a fuss about.

"The next thing we were capsized. Both of us grabbing at the hull where there was nothing really to hold on to. Now, we weren't in some fucking canoe. I call it a skiff but there were six rowlock sockets. We could have sat another oarsman amidships—no sweat.

"Neither of us had stood up. I've gone over it a million times. It was like some kind of evil miracle. One minute we're there straining hard over the paddles, the next in the water. I could feel the cold coming up my legs numbing like an anesthetic in hospital."

He slowed down even more. More than once I was afraid he'd gone, given up in the savagery of memory. But he was swept up now by something seemingly relentless. I don't think he could have stopped even if he'd wished to.

"I got longer arms than he had. I somehow managed to stretch up and my fingers found the keel. He called out then. I'm not sure what it was. Something to do with giving him a leg-up, maybe. Then his head went down. Bobbed up and then down again. His hair was running water and it flowed in and out of his eyes. Dolon was if anything darker than me. Now his flesh was just white. Like, bloodless?

"Then everything went black for me. I vaguely remember Dolon's mouth opening and closing, and then nothing. Nothing until I looked up at four or five faces peering down at me from where I lay on the stretcher. I told you about the infirmary where I was taken, and my possible lung infection? Before I'd gotten myself back here and started living like a semi-invalid?"

I ignored his questions as I knew he would too. I sensed he wasn't coming to the end, either. There was something he was dodging, eluding, yet the vortex of it was still tugging at him. Something that wouldn't let him go. Even so, I wasn't expecting his abrupt change of tack.

"When I was in high school in Bar Harbor we had a real nice English teacher. Miss Hopkins. She was in love with English Lit, especially poetry. You're a writer—recognize where this comes from?

" 'Now fades the last long streak of snow/Now burgeons every maze of quick/About the flowering squares, and thick/By ashen roots the violets blow./

" 'Now rings the woodland loud and long,/The distance takes a lovelier hue,/And drowned in yonder living blue/the lark becomes a sightless song.

" 'Now dance the lights on lawn and lea,/The flocks are whiter down the vale,/And milkier every milky sail/On winding stream or distant sea.'

"That's just a few verses but a lot more than that came back to me when I thought I was drowning and Dolon really was. Know who wrote it?"

I remained silent.

"Alfred Lord Tennyson. IN MEMORIAM. Miss Hopkins made us learn great big chunks by heart. I guess they don't do that anymore."

I was secretly glad Miss Hopkins hadn't made her pupils learn by heart *all* of *In Memoriam*. But I needn't have worried. The stanzas led inexorably onwards.

"Dolon was the the old gal's favorite. He knew all the poems she suggested. Then he was the brightest student at Bar Harbor High. Those kids that didn't like him—and they didn't like any of us Greeks anyway—called him a brown-nose. He sure wasn't the happiest kid. I backed him up. I really did. But it wasn't much use. He sniveled a lot. Then, when he started to find out about himself—sex and that—things only got worse.

"Then we went to college—he was at Harvard and I went to Boston U. He still had problems, in spite of his academic record. It was always the same. He had a real fuck-up of a love affair. But I won't go into that."

Why wouldn't he? Did he think I hadn't guessed? All this about the two of them and nary a woman in sight? I was just about to throw him a spar to climb on when he answered my unwritten question. Or rather, made it redundant.

"Dolon, you silly little curly-haired bastard! You thought I could save you, give you my hand on that slippery hull and lift you to the keel with me, but I couldn't. It wasn't the cold Charles River that numbed me, Dolon; it was you. You, in your stupid needing, froze me. Made me shiver so hard when you screamed my name, poured out all that stuff, I couldn't help trembling so hard that as you started towards me, the boat rocked and you with it. There in the water, in the splashing and gasping, I watched you accept your fate. I didn't see you drowning.

I saw you searching for the peace of sleep in those rolling brown waters of the river. Of course you raised your arm, of course you clutched at me. But those were just automatic reactions, Dolon. If I pushed you away it was only the better for you to accept what had to happen. I knew who you were, you see. I know that it was nothing to do with your sick love for me but with what the Iliad says that Odysseus saw must be your end. Odysseus and—his comrade—who together believed you must return again to the soul of the sea."

I sat hunched tight in expectancy in my computer study, hearing first the clock-ticking seconds and then my lover—not at all absent—turn heavily in sleep in the adjacent bedroom. Staring at the final words I imagined small beads of water gathering there on the screen from "the soul of the sea." Surely, they were the tears of Diomedes weeping regret.

NOWHERE IS
FAR ENOUGH

As usual with me it was late at night. The month was November and there was a storm howling outside my study window—whipping up the edge of the Pacific to an angry spume which splattered against the rocks below Point Grey a few yards beyond our front yard.

In recent weeks I had considerably extended my range on the Internet. No longer content with Canadian encounters, I had first roamed the United States, then Mexico and Brazil, and had just begun touring European countries with such things as the relay chat, where several people can be talking and listening at once, and—perhaps even more often—one-on-one conversations with individuals.

The latter is my natural habitat and when I encountered Jason McGalen I was soon glad that it was. Jason certainly asked a lot of questions but I quickly learned he was far more concerned to impart information about his dark self than he was to absorb what a cautious Davey Bryant was prepared to yield. At first, though, it was mainly hint and suspicion, nuance and insinuation.

"You've never been here in Scotland, then?"

"Only as far as Gretna Green. A friend drove us up the few miles from Carlisle. And as a small boy my parents took me to Glasgow to visit a doctor and his family who vacationed in Cornwall each year."

"But not Inverness or Oban. You don't know the Highlands?"

"I've seen pictures of The Glens. And The Lochs, and red deer coming down through the mist to drink. Oh, and Balmoral—and the Highland Games, of course."

"I'm not thinking of anything like that. Not those kinds of games, either. Just things to keep yourself amused, let's say."

I contributed nothing to the screen we shared. I knew he'd elaborate without prompting. That's something one learns from wandering around the Internet a few times.

"Not too many people live round here outside Nairn. This is Macbeth country. You remember Cawdor? The castle's not too far away. The hills are almost deserted country where I live. Mind you, there's things you can do up here you'd most likely not be doing elsewhere. Things you wouldn't want to share with others. Not necessarily, that is. This is a great part of the world for the private person. The very private person. Do you value your privacy, Davey Bryant?"

I wondered whether he had a Scottish brogue.

"Very much so, Jason. I have to admit that I also enjoy talking to other people, though. Such as your good self, for instance."

Somehow he seduced me into also using rather pompous language. "This is the first time I've ever managed to contact someone as far from British Columbia as northern Scotland. It sounds quite fascinating. Lots of Canadians have Scottish roots. But what about you, Jason? Are you a farmer in those lonely hills? Or a veterinarian maybe? We have seen the TV series ALL CREATURES GREAT AND SMALL over here. Is your life anything like that?"

He ignored all these questions. "I understand there are thirty million of us using the system. Yet I have a total sense of solitude with you, Davey. There are just the two of us, alone on the electronic highway. I like that. It's like looking up at the stars. I think I'm in love with loneliness. Can you understand what I'm saying?"

I made some rapid calculations. I estimated it must be around mid-morning his time. He could see no stars. And given it was the month of November, the weather was probably pretty bleak up there. I imagined great grey clouds sweeping in over the Hebrides from a storm-wracked Atlantic—a sort of eastern echo to what the wind and the rain were doing outside my window.

"I find the act of writing is a solitary business, Jason. But I can't say I actually feel lonely." I didn't add that my roommate was asleep in an adjacent room and that we shared the house with two dogs and a cat. When I craved solitude for my thoughts, even relief from my lover, I roamed the deserted beach below our clifftop.

"I cannot see the stars for the storm clouds," I typed. "How is your weather? I guess it is mid-morning for you."

Again he disregarded my questions. He probably thought them childish, at best frivolous. In any case, I was fast learning that Jason sailed the seas via his own charts, towards his own preconceived objectives.

"Are you a tall man?" he asked next.

"Average or just over," I replied guardedly. "Why?"

"Do you ever commit the sin of Onan? You recall Onan, I presume. That's to say Genesis, chapter thirty-eight, verses eight and nine?"

I confessed I did not.

Jason duly enlightened me by quoting: "And Judah said unto Onan, Go in unto thy brother's wife and perform the duty of an husband's brother unto her, and raise up seed to the brother. And Onan knew that the seed should not be his; and it came to pass, when he went in unto his brother's wife, that he spilled it on the ground, lest he should give seed to his brother."

I was impressed by his prodigious feat of memory but was not about to declare it. "Is that all?" I asked facetiously.

"Is it not enough, my friend? It is the hallowing of masturbation."

"I would've thought it was more like a condemnation of incest."

"Is there anything more commonly practiced that's more festooned with taboo? The hairs on the hand? The crumbling of the mind?"

He wasn't going to get me down his track so easily. Jason wasn't the only one who could be bullheaded. "Of course, incest isn't so popular nowadays but I don't think that was always the case. So TV tells us that every TV starlet in North America has been fucked by her Daddy but when I lived in France it was the boys who'd been seduced by their mamas. Trouble is, which country do you believe?"

"Do you ever stroke yourself? What they call in this country the lonely vice?"

I began to feel ever more wicked. "Is that so? I thought that it was all joint jack-offs in British schools. So we read, anyway."

"Jack-off would be the same as toss-off or wank-off?" Jason asked. "I'm not familiar with the term." Then before I could come up with a further wisecrack or deliberate misunderstanding of what he put on the screen, he added: "I am familiar with the practice, though."

I was awaiting something like that. I could see exactly where he was going. I sighed inwardly and let him carry on. This was the kind of thing that could always happen on the Internet. Why, they'd already discovered porn rings and heavy sex chat was a constant my friend Walter had told me, especially with some of the university talk groups in the States. Only this didn't go quite as I'd anticipated.

"One thing about self abuse is that it's safe. At least you can trust your own body."

I changed my mind, and decided to take one more chance to deflect him from just talking dirty on my screen as he poured out his frustrations. "Funny you should say that. I was talking to a psychiatrist at the university here recently and he told me the campus police had told him that the incidence of masturbation in the stalls of the toilets always rose during exam time. Like periods of uncertainty and an unknown future led students to go in for something that was always safe with expected results—in terms of their own bodies? Like a jack-off in the can was at least safe."

"I always thought SHE was safe. Loyal with her body, that is. But it wasn't so. Even after the child it was just as before. Our interchange constant, the mix of our several moistures. Oh, hers was such a pure looking body . . . lovely white skin . . . so infinitely soft and supple. But it was all a lie, Davey Bryant. It was the Devil's fabrication on her lying lips, the flesh of a slut she offered—a whore masquerading as my wife and the mother of my son. Well, I wasn't content with Onan's solution. Sure, when my suspicions were realized and I caught them writhing in God's holy place, I crept away to cast my seed upon the ground. But that bitch needed more than just my denial of my sperm in her as punishment. In my anguish I would have sought solace elsewhere for the ache in my groin, the hardness that would not go away. But the pain of her treachery, the deception of he whom I trusted more than anyone in the world, robbed me of any desire. I tell you I was like a eunuch! Could summon up no thought of semen as I recalled their despicable violation of the Eighth Commandment.

"As I recollected that whore's adultery with my own brother, The Reverend Angus Hypocrite, my tumescence melted over and over again. They took my balls from me as surely as if they had stolen my scalpel and severed those heavy testicles in my sleep.

"Then so very slowly, only after the years they had me locked up in that place, the Lord returned my virility. But not until I could imagine the weeds grown long on their mounds, the headstones blotched from the rain, and the mist from the sea.

"Only then did their hideous memory begin to soften in my affronted mind—to allow me the surge of life again and the milk of my manhood to return to my loins. And there's so much of it now. So much waiting to pour forth. Know what I mean, dear Davey? Can you visualize me, sitting there so far away? Can you see my nakedness? My desire rising so hard and stiff for an unknown body hidden by these electric agencies from my eyes? This yearning curve between my legs seeking flesh that cannot deceive, cannot cuckold its innocence or frustrate its insistent hunger?"

I could and I couldn't of course. Just as I wanted and did not want. Frozen in dilemma I just hung in there, wishing for things I didn't wish to hear.

The screen went suddenly blank. I guessed my invisible Scotsman had reached a climax in what he wished to say and what he was doing as accompaniment to the spurt of his words. But as I reached forward slowly to switch off my screen, to sit there in darkness for a little while and ponder the pathos of the Internet, the screen sprang alive again with a stark message phased in ungentle and urgent capitals.

WE HERE AT THE ST. LAWRENCE INSTITUTE FOR THE SICK OF MIND APOLOGIZE FOR THE UNLAWFUL USE OF OUR INTERNET FACILITIES. WE TRUST NO OFFENCE HAS BEEN GIVEN AND OFFER ASSURANCE THAT NOTHING OF THE KIND WILL HAPPEN IN THE FUTURE—THE MEDICAL FACULTY AND STAFF.

LONG AFTER HEMLOCK

"Can I tell you about someone I know here in Portland? He's gotten himself into something of a mess. The guy's in real trouble."

I sat before the computer as these words came up on my monitor. I eased my bum back on my swivel chair. I had a pretty good idea from past experience as to whom that "someone" might be. I also anticipated that it would take some time for my correspondent to reveal his identity.

"Fire away! It's also only one a.m. here in Vancouver. I decided I couldn't sleep for a while. So take as long as you like."

He didn't ask who I was, what I did, or even whether I was man or woman. Then I guessed whatever was eating him pretty much crowded out everything else. He didn't take long to confirm the impression.

"My friend is a city councillor. Very well known locally. Very high-profile. He's what you might call an educator, though he doesn't teach. Officially that is. He has a Ph.D. from Stanford. Used to teach at Berkeley for several years before coming up here and semi-retiring.

"He's gotten quite ill, you see. He was never exactly a healthy man—far too overweight for that, what with his enormous paunch. He once told me that even as a kid he had fat thighs and pudgy little hands. Anyway he got this illness—I think it's a form of lupus? It certainly doesn't help his appearance with his neck all thick and swollen up and his face suppurating. Jesus! He sometimes looks just awful!"

"Those things never help," I put in diplomatically, "especially when you've got something else bothering you."

"Bothering, you say! My friend faces the possibility of years in jail! Worse than that. Other inmates are likely to kill him when they discover what he's in for."

I think he expected me to jump in and ask what the crime was. But I didn't bother. Instinct told me he'd come up with that anyway. And why risk getting it wrong and embarrassing the both of us?

"He lives in this great big house with an old mother in her nineties. It's really huge. You could call it a mansion and in fact it's the old family home. I mention that because of the kids—his students, that is. They follow him around like as if he were Bo-peep and they were his little lambs. Some of them crash overnight. Turn up at meals, camp out on that enormous lawn. Neighbors have complained of the noise and I think the cops were called in once. But that's not where the problem is really coming from. If you ask me his enemy is that goddamned Teachers' Federation. They hate his guts for teaching without a fee."

"It's a bit odd, isn't it?" I wrote. "I mean, he isn't recognized by the state to teach in the school system. He is attached to no college or university. Are you saying he's a kind of educational free-lancer? If so, what age groups does he teach and how come they aren't in regular school somewhere—public or private, that is?"

The words came up on the screen much more slowly now. "I never said he WASN'T different, did I? He doesn't care where the kids come from—he doesn't even encourage them to go to him. I guess you could call it word-of-mouth. And they seem to be all ages and sizes. He says that's all right by him. He doesn't believe in what he calls 'chronological packaging.'

"They just ask him questions—any of them. Then he just stops whatever he's doing and answers them. The only thing is the answers can take up to forty minutes or more. Then all the others come around him, sit wherever they can park or stand up if there's nowhere else."

"That's it, then? You think teachers' greed is behind things?"

He didn't answer immediately and I stiffened. I had learned these tiny lapses—before the words started to trot again over the monitor—were often significant.

"Well, kind of. But there's been talk of what you might call hanky-panky. Though no doubt it's been them spreading more lies about him. Those selfish bastards would stop at nothing! A lot of it is jealousy you must understand."

"How old would these volunteer pupils of his be?"

"Like I said—they come in all ages. But mainly high-school drop-outs. And some a little older. You want ballpark? I'd say between very early teens to around twenty. I've never seen much older than that. Or younger than twelve or thirteen, for that matter."

"What precisely is your relationship with this man?" It was a question to which I was convinced I already knew the answer. His surprise response made me feel like the world's worst amateur psychologist.

"My name is Kerefon Jones and I am his best friend. I have spoken to a number of people, including such well-known educators as Dr. Allen Biades of UNESCO, Dr. Cyrus Plate of Harvard as well as the Director of Education at UCLA, Dr. Eunice Megar of Stanford, who was a colleague of my friend. All of them went out of the way to stress his brilliance as a pedagogue and total incorruptibility of character. The Bishop of California talked to me in similar vein but stressing even more his moral integrity."

"I am wondering why you are telling me all this—a complete and utter stranger."

"I don't know why. Just because you ARE a total stranger, maybe. I've told you what some of the finest educators say about this brilliant if unorthodox man. But I've also talked to a lot of legal opinion here in Portland. And to people like the editor of THE OREGONIAN. None of them have been other than gloomy over his chances in court. They're all convinced a jury will scream guilty.

"It's the times we live in, you see. The masses and the media that guide their every thought have to have fresh witchhunts every few years. Years ago it was just that—witches. More recently we've had the Jews in Europe. Since then, the Communists in this country. Now is the time for the so-called pedophiles. And let's not get too specific about the ages of the young men in question. Just be simplistic and believe ALL Jews are international mercenaries and that ALL opposed to McCarthy belonged to the Communist Party and were dying to spy for the Soviet Union.

"I have to tell you that my friend is so pure he couldn't conceive of touching an infant for sexual pleasure. Then I also have to be straight with you and say right out that he does love his students with unusual passion. Matter of fact he's fallen in love with teenagers and made no bones about it. So you can see why he doesn't stand a chance. Not in a time when 'youth' extends from, say, four or five years of age to eighteen or over. We are dealing with hysteria, you see. Tribal terror at the corruption of its young—the whole goddamned business has gotten entirely out of hand. People digging up phony memories from way back and the TV encouraging them to spew the crap out."

"But how can I possibly help?"

"You ARE helping me by letting me get it out of my system."

"You're suggesting that even sane and balanced people go overboard when this subject comes up? Are you absolutely certain that priests, doctors, teachers, and so on, are being convicted on charges stemming from memories sometimes from thirty or more years ago?"

"All that and more. What I know also is that my friend is in mortal danger."

"They're so steamed up they threaten his life?"

"He has asked me to acquire some alkaloid pills called coniine for his use. It is he who threatens his own life."

"This isn't easy to ask but I need a clearer picture. Are you in love with this man?"

"He is a genius. He is probably the greatest living teacher. He is a man of enormous moral stature. Perhaps a saint. What else can I say?"

"Whether you are in love with him."

"Love, smuv . . . I don't think I know what that overworked word means anymore. All I know is I see the possibility of grievous loss, of dreadful injustice and shame for mankind."

"Those are very strong words, my friend. Even a little pompous, if you don't mind my saying so."

"I am an electronics engineer. I am the senior partner in a highly regarded computer company in California. I stand to lose everything by fighting to clear his name. But he is the greatest man I have ever known and I am proud, incredibly proud, to call myself his disciple."

"Are you going to get him those pills?"

"A disciple doesn't question. Not a man like him, anyway."

"Then you will ensure his death. And after all the praise you have lavished upon him up and down this screen!"

"Thank you for hearing me out. You are very kind. I only wish you had known him."

I wanted to ask him more questions but didn't. Just sat there until I understood that he was not going to write any more words upon my monitor. I heard the cheap wall clock which Ken had nailed up last month ticking from the adjacent kitchen. For the first time it sounded like a death knell.

QUESTIONS AND ANSWERS

Q. I'm Artemis and I live along the Mendocino coast. What's your name?

A. Mine is Davey—and you've reached me in Vancouver, British Columbia.

Q. You mean you're not here in California? But the letters "CA"?

A. Stand for Canada.

Q. Is that so? Do you work these machines for a living? You seem so expert. I'm afraid I'm a hopeless amateur. I'm also a widow.

A. I'm not a travel agent. I'm a writer. TV scripts, magazine articles, that kind of thing.

Q. How thrilling! Though a bit hair-raising for your wife, I should think. I mean the uncertainty. . . .

A. I'm not married.

Q. Is that so? How very interesting. One meets so few married men on this Internet. I think it is the playground of the young.

A. I am not so young.

Q. But young enough to read these little words on your screen. Young enough to manipulate all this complicated process. I imagine you enjoy good health. You sound so sprightly! Are you a man of many tastes?

A. Many tastes. I enjoy meeting strangers—especially one degree removed from reality as we are able to do on the Internet. I am less happy with personal encounter. A bit anti-social I'm afraid. This technology was made for the likes of us.

Q. Oh, come! I don't think you are one bit anti-social. Your words brim with curiosity. Do you travel much? Are you familiar with this neck of the woods?

A. You flatter me. Yes, I have been to Fort Ross. I love that little wooden fort built by the Russian fur traders. I almost bought a house some years ago in Mendocino. It was octagonal and Victorian. But last time I visited there I couldn't find it. I think the township cleared all the buildings that were right on the edge of the ocean. It made me feel as if part of my life had been bulldozed into oblivion.

Q. I live in an area known as the Sea Ranch. It is very wild and lovely. We came up here when my husband retired from his optical business. Do you come down here via I-5 or take the coastal route? The latter is much slower, of course, the scenery so much more rewarding. Do you respond to spectacular views? I am a complete slave to the picturesque!

A. It is indeed a lovely coastline, especially when there is no fog. We drive south as far as Roseburg, Oregon, where we stay overnight. Then we just drive on a few miles south to Coos Bay. The dogs love the beaches. This must be boring you.

Q. To the contrary. You make it all sound so easy. But I suspect there is great preparation. I get so flustered and lose pieces of paper with addresses and phone numbers on them. I rarely leave here now unless it is to drive south to the city to take care of some business or other relating to the optical stores. You speak of "we." Is it a friend who accompanies you and your dogs on these delightful expeditions?

A. Often there are friends. Once it was my mother and my aunt. But they are now dead. I have traveled alone but that is not always satisfactory. At a certain age I think it prudent to travel with a companion. One hears terrible tales of violence driving the highway. Life has changed so.

Q. Which is why we choose this electronic highway, don't you think? I am surprised that there are not more mature people using it in this fashion. It is wasted on the young! Do you live alone as I do, Mr. Davey?

A. I mentioned the dogs, I think. And by the way, "Davey" doesn't take a prefix.

Q. Are you always so stately with your language, Davey? Or is it just this form of communication that inspires you? Yes, you did mention the dogs but not your entire domestic circumstance. There! I am doing the same as you. I have never used "domestic circumstance" before. Actually it is rather fun isn't it? I mean, like wearing masks at a masquerade ball or something.

A. It is certainly a change from my TV scripts and that kind of stuff. Perhaps we use the Internet as a holiday from reality.

Q. Oh, I don't think so. We are being very real this evening. I mean two strangers talking of their past lives, and the awful sense of loss inspired by the razing of familiar buildings in our lives. Is that not reality at its harshest? You cannot know it but when you confessed the loss of the octagonal house at the ocean's edge you brought tears to my eyes.

A. That was certainly not my intention. I have no wish to hurt. There is enough of that about without me turning the electronic highway into a hazardous highway!

Q. You are indeed deft with words! Is that a natural trait or the result of superior education? I am an uneducated woman although I attended Mills College in Oakland. My husband did too much of my thinking for me. Now I regret it. But here alone at the Sea Ranch there is much to regret—though I do try and keep negative thoughts at bay. It is not my natural temperament, you see. Are you what might be called a jolly man? Or does despondency claim you from time to time?

A. You have so many questions! I cannot remember them all when they come in such swift succession. I suppose I've always had a flair for words though my education wasn't all that exceptional. And I cannot claim to be free of sad or distressing thoughts from time to time. Then I think I'm just run-of-the-mill as far as the gamut of emotions go.

Q. That comforts me. Don't you think that sharing is the secret? That as long as we can share both joy and misery we can survive? I can assure you that is the true cost of widowhood. The absence of another pair of ears and the comfort of another's words. You get used to it of course. The original pain abates. But not the pain of no one left to listen. That never goes away. We go to great lengths to deal with it. I, for instance, make common cause with several other husbandless women here at the Sea Ranch. But we really have nothing but our sense of loss in common. If Basil were alive I know very well I would hardly give them the time of day. Does that make me a cynic, Davey?

A. In my book it just makes you very human. It also makes me appreciate the fact that I know no widows. Only a handful of divorcées of a certain age. And they are not the same.

Q. We all live in ghettoes nowadays, don't you think? Only I have to be careful. I heard someone say in our general store the other day that you could tell how old people are by the amount of time they spend grumbling. I don't want to be labeled like that, do you?

A. I hate all kinds of labels. If you knew my background you'd understand why. But it isn't just the old. Even my own kind are constantly labeling—that's to say defining and therefore confining.

Q. May I ask what kind is that? Is it possible for you to tell me, do you think?

A. We are coming to the limitations of the Internet. There are only the words as signs. If we were physically facing each other I could read your face for comprehension, for sympathy. There would be other icons to tell me if I could go further or not. A raising of the brow, movement at the temples, even a down-turning of the mouth.

Q. But we do not have that luxury, do we? So this way is perhaps more risky. But where would we be without risk? It's like dieting.

Skeletons are never obese. And people in coffins don't worry about taking chances. There are none to take anymore.

A. You have a point. But I'm still not sure I'm close enough to death to be persuaded by indiscretion.

Q. I am sixty-nine and have "the big C." It is not fear but modesty that prevents me from naming the specifics. Can you understand now why I am in love with risk and so want to hold hands with the human race?

A. I am seventy-one and am homosexual. I have mild diabetes but I have eluded AIDS, which has taken so many, many friends. Well, there you have it, you persistent woman! I have now told a perfect stranger in California things about myself that my mother never knew at her death aged ninety-four.

Q. So there we are, indeed. We now know some very heavy things about each other. On second thought I am not sure this medium is the best way to communicate. Beyond a certain level, that is. Don't you think it could so easily lead to misuse?

A. I have never doubted it. But you exalt risk. I cannot see electronic risk as different from any other. In fact you are a great persuader, Artemis. I don't think that I will ever be quite the same on the Internet again. I am grateful for that. In fact I have to thank you.

Q. I have always wondered about people who remain bachelors all their lives. What is the term they use? Lifestyle. Men and women who choose a childless lifestyle.

A. That is one way of putting it. Though I would quarrel with the verb "choose" as in my life there has been no question of choice as to my basic sexual identity. But I have always wondered about widows and widowers. My mother once told me that happy marriages led to remarriage—following the death of one of the partners. Though she did not do so when my father died. On the other hand I have heard women say that such precious experiences should never be duplicated. That, of course, was the view of Queen Victoria after the demise of Albert.

Q. It is not my view. Perhaps over this and other things we must agree to differ in our computer conversation. Can we not just say that we are just ships passing in the night?

A. Yes indeed, we are ships passing in the night for I can see we are headed for different harbors.

KAN AND MAC

Right off on the Internet she told me her name was Kan "with a K" and that she had a brother named Mac. In amused response I told her I was Davey Bryant and immediately turned my lover into an honorary brother and said his name was Ken.

"We live in Berkeley. Where are you?"

"Vancouver, B.C. Right up the coast from you."

"Do you live with your parents?"

"They are both dead now. In any case, they lived in Cornwall in southwest Britain. That's where I grew up."

"Lucky you!"

"Growing up in Cornwall? Yes, it was a very special place for me. Still is."

"I meant having dead parents."

I'll admit that rocked me rather. However, I wasn't about to admit it. "Am I to gather your parents are alive and kicking? And could it be you are living under their roof?"

Somehow I inferred she was quite young. At least young enough to be devoid of prevarication—that's to say, she was really up front with her questions and answers. She went on to live up to my assessment.

"Certainly you could call them 'kicking.' My Dad in particular. He's a cop. Name of Ellis and he scares the hell out of me. Was your old man a s.o.b.? How did he get on with your brother Ken? Mine hates Mac. Then he hates me even worse. Thinks we always gang up on him."

She was going a little fast for my taste—in spite of her refreshing candor. "Are you still in high school, Kan?"

"Hell no, I'm at Mills. This is my sophomore year. Mac is at Berkeley so he's nearby. He's a Senior. We see each other every day. We're thinking of moving permanently together into this place. That would be really neat but if either of us just mentions it our Dad starts to froth at the mouth. Mac says we should just go ahead and do it without telling him. When we graduate we both want to go to veterinarian school. Then we could end up with a joint practice."

"Are you twins or something?"

"Not twins. Just something, I guess. What about you and Ken?"

"What about us?"

"Well, like does he live close to you? And are you real buddies as well as being brothers?"

That wasn't so hard to answer. "Ken and I are really close. As a matter of fact we live together here. He's a prof at the university. I'm a freelance writer."

I decided that was enough info to hand out. Besides, Kan intrigued me. I wanted to know more.

"Is your Dad a cop on the beat? You'd think he'd be proud of a son and daughter both in college."

"He's the Chief of Police. He's also a Stanford graduate. Nothing impresses him."

I tried a different tack. "You haven't said much about your mother."

"What is there to say? Her name is Enid. She and my father keep having kids. Six to date. Otherwise she's completely uninteresting. Let's talk about something else, Davey-from-Vancouver."

"Do you have any suggestions?"

There was a pause before I received a response.

"I'm frightened. I think he's found out."

I replied very carefully. "Who are you frightened of, Kan? And what has he found out?" I had a pretty good idea of the answer to both questions, but I wanted confirmation. Put crudely, to cover my ass before continuing with some rather dicey suppositions. I waited patiently.

The blank space on my screen remained so. After some time I felt restless, wondering whether my attempt to nail her down had in fact scared her off. I tried something else.

"Is the Internet the only way you can go? I mean, isn't there something closer to home and help than us sharing this little screen?"

That did the trick.

"I don't want anyone around here to know. If you'd said you were from San Francisco I'd have signed off immediately. Dad's got contacts all over the Bay Area. Police chiefs do. It wouldn't be the first time he's tried to trap us. I mean, he even tiptoed upstairs hoping to find us together. This is an old Maybeck home. There are lots of rooms and lots of dark corners. But the stairs creak, too. That's what saved us the first time. But last night I swear he saw us. I whispered to Mac but he just plumped up his pillow and turned over. Told me I was imagining things. But when Dad called this morning after breakfast I knew something was up. In the first place he wasn't supposed to know the phone number. Mom promised not to tell him. Then he said something about Tunnel Road and I knew at once he'd found out where we were living. I've tried to call Mac several times all day to warn him but I can't locate him on campus. I just pray to God he doesn't go home like he'd promised Mom he'd do today. But I don't dare call her in case you-know-who answers. Dad threatened to kill him last week. That wasn't even because he'd learned that Mac and I were already living together though he started off on that. It was when Mac told him to keep his cool—and suggested that our brother Al and our sister Sally were thinking of moving out of the house and setting up joint shop together as soon as they were through high school—that's when he really went mad. Said he'd kill either or both of us if he ever found out what he suspected was true."

"And if that's what I'm thinking, Kan, you could both get thrown in jail. There's a law about brothers and sisters, you know. They call it incest."

Her words flooded the screen—I don't know whether from relief that it was now out in the open or that I'd touched a raw nerve. In any event, a torrent of wildly romantic declarations over her brother Mac now flowed. They had loved one another, she wrote, in "that special way" since puberty. That they had enjoyed each other as "husband and wife" since before they were through high school, and that their passion for one another was equal and paramount. Knowing that their love was "clean" and unequivocal—in spite of the world's taboos over such affection—they had informed their mother they were in love. She hadn't reacted much one way or the other at the time, they'd both felt.

"Then, with kids crawling all over her on that great bed of theirs and her belly huge with another impending, I guess she had other things on her mind," Kan added ruefully. That had made them somewhat careless, she admitted. With incredible naïveté they'd acted as if Ralph Waldo Emerson were right in observing that all mankind loves a lover—as if the kind of lover and the nature of the love were immaterial.

I was tempted to indicate that she was revealing herself to a gay man whose relationship with his partner was also regarded by the world at large as perverted and immoral, but she afforded me no space to insert such encouragement. Nothing was about to impede her outpouring; to slacken the swelling amalgam of desperate love for her brother and the mortal fear of her father that now obviously possessed her.

"I am sure he is in the house. I can hear him. They aren't Mac's footsteps down there. Do you know what Mac said Dad told him? That I had to die. That was the price I had to pay for what I'd done."

Now her words seemed to drag a little, but they still kept coming across my pale gray monitor. "But my father is very generous, Davey. He told my darling brother that of course I had a choice. I could either take my own life— he'd send me a gun to do that. Or he'd proudly fulfill the role of executioner of his disgusting daughter."

I managed to squeeze in a sentence. "Sounds as if it is he who's the screwed-up one—not you, Kan."

But that proved my final contribution.

"It's him! And he's coming up those stairs again, just like before. Only this time I know he's going to make me choose. What shall I do? Mac, where are you?"

There her words stopped, burned there on my screen until—God knows when later—Ken made me switch the computer off.

There is a postscript of sorts. Ten days later a friend sent me a clipping from the *Oakland Tribune*. He was directing my attention to an article on the artist Richard Diebenkorn whom he knew I admired greatly. Idly scanning the whole sheet he had torn from the paper I chanced upon the following:

"The body of Kan King, twenty-one-year-old daughter of Berkeley Police Chief Ellis King and Enid King, was discovered yesterday with two gunshot wounds to the head. Officials say they are currently calling it a suicide. The deceased was found by her elder brother, Macareus. She leaves both parents, and five younger brothers and sisters. Funeral arrangements to be announced."

JUST CALL ME "THERESA"

God knows why I decided that night to pretend on the Internet I was a woman. It wasn't as if I were into drag, cross-dressing, or any of those things.

So you can see that this sudden decision to change sexual identity on the Internet was an idiosyncratic one, to put it mildly. But the results of that decision were even more strange—as I was to shortly find out.

I had been talking with a very dull Swede from Lund whose desire to learn English torpedoed all attempts at general conversation. So that when blithely asking about the breeding habits of feral reindeer in Lapland (a topic on which I was woefully ignorant) the response was how did one use the subjunctive in English? Or in seeking information on whether gay life flourished in Stockholm, was asked what *ambidextrous* meant.

At first, in mild boredom, I asked him the Swedish translation for "the missionary position," but when that drew a blank I asked him what was the status of single women like myself in Sweden. That at least brought relief from his efforts at linguistic self-improvement on the screen before me.

It also cranked him up again (he'd already revealed *his* gender) and made him change his tack. We immediately departed the world of grammar and syntax to enter one that surpassed divisions of language and was common to the whole human race.

"You are here on the Internets so often? Looking around, yes?"

"Very often," I said, wishing I could make my words sound husky on this harsh little screen. "It is how I spend much of my time."

As they are wont, snippets from movies swirled about my mind—rather like the screen-saver images which we computer folk have come to employ. If I couldn't always remember my heroine's lines I was only too pleased to extemporize. It was this device I drew upon now with my Swede.

"I am looking for the right kind of man. So much of life is a search." That was a highly garbled version of something poorly remembered from over sixty years ago: Elisabeth Bergner's starring performance as a beautiful young mother with an illegitimate baby, which had won my nine-year-old heart and lingers there to this day. I decided to extemporize much further as I eased into my role. The only pity was that the monitor didn't allow me to reveal my pretty Austrian accent.

"I am already now nineteen and my father still will not allow me to go ashore from this island. He is not a cruel man but he is so afraid of my meeting men that I have to mope here in the candlelight and imagine my own Flying Dutchman! It's only because he sees me as so much more beautiful than I am. Just because I am a brunette and have inherited my mother's violet eyes. Papa calls me his Elizabeth Taylor—foolish man. But I am so bored here as I look across at the mainland just a few miles a mile away. I have only the Internet to take me away. I wonder if Prince Charming comes down the electronic highway in these modern times?"

"You sit in candlelight? Does your computer run on the batteries, then? That is most unusual, no?" God, those Swedes are a prosaic lot.

"We have our own power plant here on the island. Then, Papa is very rich. The locals call him Croesus. And that's not just because there's a town near here called Sardis."

The allusion was lost on my dumb Swede. But I guess the musk of my words was still operating. "You are a virgin, then? And I do not know your name, young lady. Mine is Sven. Sven Olaffson at your service."

"Theresa." I decided to give up my favorite *Ver is my babee?* line of Miss Bergner's and encourage him. "And Theresa has only ever dreamed of men. There are none here on the island."

"You say none? That is so hard to believe, Theresa."

I could only imagine the doubt trembling his words but decided to act upon the supposition, and retract somewhat. "None that my father might fear. They are all so old—or so young," I added, hoping that sounded suitably enigmatic.

He abruptly changed tack. "What are you looking for in a man, Theresa? Tell me your visions of what the ideal man should be."

I embarked on a congenial journey. "I would prefer someone a little older than me—say, in his mid-twenties, or even a bit more. I want a man who smiles gently and has lots of patience with a girl who doesn't know very much but is completely willing to learn. Such a man should also have a practical side and know how to fix things. If he can handle a boat and understands the sea, all the better. But that is very important in these parts, as you can imagine."

As I drew breath for a second bout of imaginative steam his words started to hop across my screen. "They are coincidences but I possess many of these things you mention, Theresa. I cannot claim the encyclopedic nautical knowledge but I can make sail a small sailboat and often do near Lund in the seas out of Malmo. I am Practical Man, even if I am University Teacher."

So that's what the guy did. I wondered how old he was. He didn't keep me waiting for long.

"I shall soon be moving to Uppsala. That is, north of Stockholm. I will be in the theology school at the university, as I am here. I will also be assistant pastor in the parish so I will be a busy man, you will

understand? After all this studying I will now start the looking around
for—a helpmate? I shall be looking for a wife, Theresa. I am also very
moderns and come on this program of the computer looking for right
persons as well as improving my English. It is important you see,
Theresa, that she is moderns too. I am of the Swedish Lutheran Church
but we are of the new generation. We are not any more as our Ingmar
Bergman put in such motion picture as WINTER LIGHT. That was indeed
the past. Those days are truly over for the pastors, for the Church, for
Sweden."

I forgot my assumed role. "Even so, I just loved THE SEVENTH SEAL
and WILD STRAWBERRIES. Oh yes, THE VIRGIN SPRING and that weird
one—THE SILENCE."

That comment brought just that—silence, at least momentarily.
"You know our Bergman well. That is something for a young girl on
an island. So many Bergman films. So many remembered titles!"

I was getting testy. "I said I was nineteen, Sven. Not nine! And I
have been a movie buff since childhood. We have a super Memorex
video player and Dad gets me several videos a week to watch. We
islanders are not ignorant even if our social lives aren't exactly
hectic."

It occurred to me that I probably wasn't sounding exactly like a
nineteen-year-old virgin. But what the heck—his English wasn't all that
hot, either.

"I did not mean to disturb your integrity, Theresa. It was that I was
impressed by your encyclopedic knowledge of our Swedish filmmaker.
There are not so many peoples with such knowledge. Would you have
photographs of you and do you use the fax?"

I had and I didn't. I promised to send him a snap by regular mail.

"I would love to show you Sweden if you to take the vacations here.
It is a beautiful land full of lakes and sea. I have always thought that
Canada was much like this country. If you was to think of vacation here
I would be sincerely delighted to be of assistance. I am full of loneliness

at these times and it is this beautiful summer months that I must make the big decisions for life as I make my move to Uppsala."

This was getting far too heavy, in spite of the fractured English. Gritting teeth, I returned to my male gender. "Sven, I have been deceiving you, I'm afraid. I am a man and not a young girl. I am sorry if I have strung you along. That is, given you a false impression. The Internet system permits rather nasty jokes and I am truly sorry if my certainly misplaced sense of humor has embarrassed you. And if I'm being quite honest with you now, I must also add that I am a gay man and that is what I thought you were too when we began this chat. It is an assumption I have made too often when having this kind of Internet chat. Though 'chat' is rather a silly word in this context, isn't it? It is sometimes a real peeling off of skins."

I awaited his reply with some trepidation as I felt my pulse race from the effort of confession. But I needn't have worried. He was long gone I suspect before I finished that last painful spiel.

DOWN ON THE RANCH

You don't think of cowboys when you sail down the Information Highway from Vancouver on the wings of the Internet. Not that Poz, as he called himself, was exactly a cowpoke. He didn't write like one though he didn't write exactly like a college graduate either. In fact his style varied startlingly from the carefully correct to the highly vernacular. Something I'd never met before on the Internet and not often since.

He told me he was originally from Monterey in California and been a fisherman before his Greek-born wife, remembering her childhood, got frightened by the constant earth tremors around nearby Hollister (which he oddly claimed to actually enjoy) and persuaded them to move far inland to the cattle country east of Grass Valley.

But he didn't begin with the geography of his upbringing and current life. To the contrary.

"Do you have a family up there in Vancouver?" he asked abruptly.

"My mother used to visit and that was a precious thing. But she is long dead and the others don't come. They live thousands of miles away. In Cornwall. That suits me, too. You are also an emigrant? Your family is back in Europe?"

"No. They're everywhere. Only they don't know Amphy and me is up here in the Gold Country. If they ever do then we move on again. Point is, I don't trust my father nor my two brothers. I know goddamn well they's responsible for the fact one of my kids—well, let's say Trev has learning problems. Can't prove it, of course, but I know he's never been the same since he fell off that pony when staying at Dad's place as a little fella when Amphy—his Mom—was sick and I was out fishing off the Farallons. My other son, Cy, is now part-blind and I blame my brothers for that, too. I swear they did something to him when he was just a tad. Can't prove that, either."

I was intrigued by his gross misfortunes, not least because I saw Vancouver as a place of refuge from the thrall of those who would lay claim on me by ties of blood. A place I could be free to have an Elkhound, a pug, and a spoiled cat without aged aunts tut-tutting about extravagance and asserting that pets had no place in the home.

"My lot aren't exactly what you might call dangerous," I confessed. "Just boring. Their horizons don't extend much beyond their waist-lines and who has slighted who in the last little while. The marvelous thing about here on the west coast is that I haven't had to inherit a single human being. Every friend is from choice—so we all meet as equals."

However, I told him I really sympathized with his family tragedy, which by comparison made my problems all so petty. But he was having none of it. "These things happen, man. Nothing you can do about it. Leastways, you don't hang around for more when you find someone working real evil on you. But other than that you just learn to live with it. Get on with life, that's what I say. We don't go in for family feuding up here. Keep to ourselves. That's why I like this Internet. You talk to who the hell you like, no strings attached.

"Not that I got too much time to spend on all this indoor stuff. We got the horses, you see. They take up most of the time for all of us. Raising purebreds is a full-time business, I can tell you. There's the grazing and keeping an eye on them summer and winter. Then all the bedding and breeding. The boys help out but young Trev can only do the simpler things like cleaning out the stables, and piling up the shit. And Cy's eyes aren't good for much. Bit of grooming's all I can get out of him—if I stick a curry comb in his hand and guide it to the mane. So, all in all, neither of them is up to much, come to that."

"Mind if I say something?" I asked, the anonymity of my monitor prompting me to a boldness I certainly wouldn't have employed in a face-to-face situation.

"Fire away, Buster. The ranch is quiet and the family is all asleep. I got all the time I want. After all, this is my relaxation. That's why I took the computer course over in Sacramento in the first place."

"That's it, Poz. You just don't seem the type. I don't know how old you are but obviously you aren't a mere kid. And then the fishing and farming—it somehow doesn't all add up to computers and e-mailing and that kind of stuff."

"No one ever told you it takes all sorts to make a world?"

"I'm sorry. I didn't mean anything personal. That's not my way."

"Seeing as we have things in common, no offense taken. Fucking relatives is the root of all evil, if you ask me. Wanna help me? Give help to an old fisherman who has heartache for the open seas? I guess it's late and I'm feeling low. But if you wanted to help out a guy who has the most evil kin known to man and more—well, I don't mind telling you I'd be grateful."

This outburst scared me, frankly. I'd heard about nuts on the Internet but never panhandlers. Any minute now, I thought, he's going to hit me for a loan. I sought my words very carefully.

"But Poz, I'm well over a thousand miles away from you. And I know nothing about farming—even though I was raised on a farm. What I am is just an impecunious writer. Of course, if there was some kind of way. . . . If I could really be of assistance. But I'm not even a family man, you see. I know nothing of marriage, of having children. Just a bit about pets."

"No one's asking you for anything like that. It was just a bit of support over the airwaves is all I was asking. But don't you worry your sweet self! I never begged nor borrowed in my life. You just ask anyone who knows me and they will tell you old Poz has never bowed the knee to anyone."

"It's obvious I've upset you. I am sorry for that. I guess we're all something of novices with this technology. We've all got to learn a whole new set of manners."

"I tell you what I gotta learn, my friend. And that is not to trust humans but stay with what I know. Once it was the great creatures of the ocean. Now? Well, now it's my horses. They don't let you down, you see. They aren't treacherous. Let me tell you something about my real friends out here at the PH Ranch. Know what those initials stand for? Bet you don't. I dug it up in the Grass Valley Library, of all places. That's Greek for Poseidon Horses and that's what I stand for. Got the horses and Amphy's folks in the same breath, see? That got me started on the names. Pelias, Pegasus, and Perseus. They are my studs. Then I got the brood mares: Periboia, Ephialtes, and Pelopia, Aithra, Boutes, and Euryale. And I tell you, fella, there ain't a one of them I'd exchange for a goddamn human. Take Pelopia. I love that mare—the gentlest creature I've ever met. You know the dumbest bit of cussing there is? To call someone a horse's ass! Why there ain't nothing more beautiful than the ass on Pelopia. All lovely curve and as smooth as the sand on Half Moon Bay when the tide's out. I won't go into her other details save to say they make the human version chickenshit in comparison. Tiny screwed-up affairs to be ashamed of compared with the pride and innocence of a horse. There's no evil over the private parts of Pelopia— or my big stallion Pegasus, come to that."

I sensed what the old man was talking about. "I couldn't agree more, Poz. There's no original sin with animals. That's why I like them around. They force you to confront innocence—after dollops of trickery, treachery and guile from our lot."

But he wasn't to be deflected. "Horses—now they're something again, son. There's the beauty and the innocence. But there is something more with them. What you might call noble. I seen it before mind. Out at sea when the great grey whales are riding the swells of Monterey Bay on their way down to Mexico for calving. First there's the setting to stick in your mind. Here it's the hills, soft as mole's fur in the January spring and as green as green. When the horses swish their plumes and munch grass in the sunset.

"On the ocean, it's different. But when those creatures sail by, so big and so quiet as they make those oily ripples. . . . Well, the horses remind me of them in some ways. They both make a man feel small and humble as you fill right up with awe. It's not all peace and quiet, mind. Let's not be sentimental about our fellow critters. I was once out there, some eight miles from the wharf in Monterey harbor. We'd sailed through the barking din of the sea lions, seen the big bulls, now dried beige in the sun, slide into the kelp from their sunbathing rocks. Then forgot about them as we watched brown pelicans flying in row formation and then saw the black and white flash of killer whales hunting.

"That was the moment my friend Tony spied what the killer whales were chasing. It was one of those massive bulls from the sea lion herd at the entrance to Monterey Harbor. He thought it had followed us hoping for fish remains from after we had trawled and picked up our nets again. By all the gods, that was a dreadful moment. One minute there was just the heaving calm, the reassuring smell of the brine and the quick flash of those black and white bodies, like huge aquatic panders, as they frolicked and broke the sea's surface. The next, after one last glimpse of the bobbing head of the frantic seal, the waters were turned to frenzy and the blue-grey ocean turned into an angry pool of crimson as those sea-wolves found their prey.

"Was it a seagull's scream or that of the hunted creature we heard? I will never know. But as we hung over the side of our craft, that circle of death frothed to a frenzy one final time—and then slowly diluted as the seas quieted and the orca pod moved on. I tell you, you don't forget things like that.

"Nor will I forget a time later, much later, when I was up on the stallion Pegasus and we come across the mountain lion. It was asleep, holed up on a slight mound and screened by a clump of sagebrush. But I knew Pegasus had scented something when he tossed back his black mane, flared his nostrils and whinnied so soft I had to strain to hear. I might as well not have held the reins or jammed into the stirrups for the next little while. That stallion took over—rose like a wild thing.

"The cougar never knew what was happening. Pegasus shot up in the air, his forelegs pawing and a deep scream now coming from that mighty throat, and I saw the gaping cuts in the cat's coat, the spurting blood turn the fur from tawny to red. What with the stallion's roar and the snarls of the cougar as it was flailed by those murderous hooves, the whole goddamned universe was forced to listen. Pegasus didn't stop stomping until there was nothing but a pile of sodden cat meat beneath him. And only then did he respond to my yanking hands and kicking feet to turn and face the ranch house—a purple smudge in the distance.

"I had more than Pegasus murdering his natural enemy to remember that day. When I got home I found Amphy running about, screaming her lungs out. That was when I learned my son was never going to see those killer whales turn the ocean red, or my great stallion destroy a mountain lion. In fact, the eye doctor in Grass Valley had told Amphy that in a matter of months the boy would scarcely know night from day."

"You've seen a great deal," I said lamely, really at a loss for words.

"I seen more than any one man should," he wrote. "I was overflowing—which is why I'm glad you heard me out. Now I'm tired. Good night, Boy!"

But perversely I wanted more. I tried vainly to raise him up again then and there in the deep watches of the night. I still try every now and then but so far with no success. But that's what draws me to him.

They don't come like that anymore—strange Poz and his awesome friends of land and sea.

FATHERS AND SONS

He called himself Ronny but I suspected right off the bat that it wasn't his real name. Not that I found that particularly surprising. Not on the Internet where people are even encouraged to use nicknames.

What was more surprising came a little later, after the usual polite preliminaries had been accomplished across our mutual screens. He'd learned that I was a Canadian living in Vancouver, and I now knew that he was born and raised in Adams, Massachusetts, although now living just west of Northampton in Florence. He added that he taught at Smith College and that he was an astronomer with a special interest in the planets Saturn and Jupiter.

At which point we moved to other matters.

"You have pets, Davey?"

"We have a Norwegian Elkhound, a cat, and a canary. Why? Do you?"

"Dalmatians. Two brood bitches and a stud at present. We usually have several more but my wife hasn't been well and as there's too much work for one, we just cut down on the kennel."

All innocuous enough, you might say—but he didn't stop his doggy talk there. "Ever show your dog?"

I was puzzled. "To whom?"

"A dog show. Like The A.K.C. at Madison Square Garden or what they call simply Cruft's in Britain? They're the two international biggies."

"No, I haven't. I went to a couple of those shows, here and in Seattle, some ten years ago when we were thinking of getting a puppy. But that's all. I'm afraid that we both found them rather boring."

"You went with your father?"

I paused for a moment but I don't think he noticed. "I went with Ken. He's my roommate."

I thought he might've picked up on that but he didn't. Instead he changed the subject in a rather odd way. "If a dog has only one testicle he can't compete. They call them monorchids. Did you know that?"

I not only didn't know, I'd never heard of the word, and told him so. He persisted with the topic.

"There's another name. Perhaps you're more familiar with it. Ever heard of cryptorchid dogs?"

Again I had to confess ignorance, adding, "Why this interest in a dog's balls, or lack of them, Ronny? It's an unusual topic."

He wasn't particularly forthcoming.

"What do you think of all this stuff they are now saying about men?"

I wasn't about to give this new Internet encounter my private thoughts about men in general or my lover in particular. He would have had to drop more than one bead to tempt me to frankness in that quarter. As it was, he hadn't provided a hint as to his own sexual propensities— and I wasn't about to regard one-balled dogs as any kind of clue.

"I'm not sure exactly what they in fact are saying about men. Is there some new theory as to where we came from?"

He patently didn't find that funny. Ignored it altogether.

"I guess you don't read the papers or watch the interviews on TV or anything. You would know if you did or if you lived here in the Lesbian Center of the Universe—with a bunch of fucking Amazons—that men are all rapists, child molesters, wife and woman beaters, and control females as the ultra-slaves of the economy. That's just for starters, Dave. Men are also the weaker species, dying earlier than women. Blood-thirsty, of course. They just love wars. And don't forget that men are all-round haters of everyone but themselves—that would include queers, of course."

It occurred to me that perhaps he hadn't been impervious to my earlier remarks about my roommate after all. "And am I to infer you think such blanket condemnation possibly a little extreme?"

"I will tell you exactly what I think. In fact that is why we are talking right now on the Internet. I could tell right off you were the kind of guy I should be talking to. A good listener, and someone who lives marginally enough to understand the problems of other people."

I must say that rang a familiar bell. It wouldn't be the first time the Internet safely concealed my ego and my frequent impatience and led people to believe that I approached saintliness in my power to be all ears to those wishing to unburden. Then this device can be quite treacherous and lead people to profound misjudgments. So if you are tempted to look for me along the electronic highway, well, you can't say you haven't been warned. . . .

But back to Ronny and his distinct peculiarities. He soon came to the first of these via his berating of feminists who sought their goals by being anti-male.

"Is your Dad still around? Like does he live near you there in Vancouver?"

I wasn't interested in whatever game he was playing. "My father's been dead a long time," I stabbed out crisply. "My mother, too. Ken and I have no relatives here. We like it that way."

"I wish that were true for me, my friend. But my father is in a nearby nursing home ever since the accident over twenty years ago. A 'vegetable' I guess you'd have to call him. Though Rhea hates it when I say so. Only he hasn't lost his memory. He knows I was driving and he still blames me for what happened."

I'm always embarrassed when people start talking too intimately about their families. I tried to dilute matters. "Rhea is your wife?"

I was soon to regret what had seemed such an innocuous question.

"I guess you could say that. We were married in a Unitarian Church in Boston."

"Congratulations!"

"Only for obvious reasons we never told the Minister we were brother and sister."

This time I prudently held my tongue—or rather refrained typing any more cute statements on the keyboard.

"Have I shocked you? It's no big deal. It's what we decided we both wanted when were quite young. Even Mom didn't make too much fuss. Then, looking back, I guess she was working to her own agenda. It was she who insisted I drive Dad that night it happened. I was only seventeen and she knew I was pissed at that party in Adams, the small hilltown where I'd been raised. Of course even she couldn't have known what was going to happen. That my Dad was going to end up a goddamn eunuch after quarreling with me in the car and trying to take the wheel from me. Or could she? Gay Teightons is one strong lady. I think it was she who has made me attracted to them. Certainly Rhea is a tough cookie too. Then sometimes I forget my wife is also my Mom's daughter. Incest makes life complicated that way."

Of course there was no way of my knowing whether he was being funny or not. And after what had happened I was not about to ask. I needn't have worried in any event. He was in full steam by this point.

"If it hadn't been for Rhea I guess I'd still be in jail. After what I did to Dad I guess I sort of fell to pieces. I dropped out of college—Amherst, that is. Then I wasn't very good with our first son, Leo. In fact Rhea got a restraining order when in temper I threw a rock at him when we were hiking in the Berkshires and nearly killed him. He was sent off to our grandparents in North Adams and I ended up in prison in Springfield. For years I wasn't allowed to see Leo—even after I was out of jail, and was living only with Rhea once more—as all the other kids—Poz and Heidi and the others, had been taken away from me, too. But even though I'm reconciled—sort of—with Leo and he has done his best to help me with the rest of the family, my Dad won't have any of it. Mom says it's best the way things are, that she's quite happy to have the old guy a neuter. She calls him her pathetic little eunuch. But then she hates him, of course. As much I'd say as he hates me for taking his manhood away. Funny, isn't it, Dave? I try to murder my son, my kids all flee from me, my wife still doesn't trust me around her kids—yet all of that has been more or less resolved. What's left is a couple of gristle pills that when push comes to shove you can live without. But the absence of those two tiny balls? Well, just ask old Uri Teightons and he'll sit up in that bed he's lived in for over twenty years, his neck wobbling like a turkey wattle, and his scraggy arms like blanched sticks shaking in rage, and curse me for every disaster in heaven and earth. You can see why I don't visit him too often—get his daughter to do that and tell him about the kids. Though that isn't always a safe thing to do."

Now I did feel it incumbent to say something.

"You don't paint a pretty picture. It is hard for an outsider to comprehend such a bleak life. So much misfortune." I warmed to my theme. (Besides, it was my turn.) "Perhaps being a Canadian, living here in Vancouver is part of the problem. So little crime, so little violence and so few guns permitted. Then throw in that there are no extremes of weather. It all tends to make us more than a bit complacent."

"You don't have old men shut up in rest-homes, railing at the world and wishing they were dead and not being forcibly kept alive."

"If so it wouldn't be because they were castrates—or that their children were sexually coupled to each other."

I thought that might shut him up, or at least get him off the topic of family onto something else, like his profession of astronomy and his interest in Jupiter and Saturn. But apart from all the information exchanged I don't think I had much sense of Ronny. At least my verbal strategy didn't appear to have the slightest impact. In fact, I was beginning to think we inhabited separate worlds. My taboos were his commonplaces, my somewhat restricted sense of family eons from his multiple and even murderous one.

That sense was then and there confirmed. "This is far from a calm place. And I'm not thinking only of one sexless old man who hates himself and tries to stir up more trouble between me and my sons. I don't trust the bitch I live with all that much—and I have a strong suspicion she is involved with the bunch of man-hating women here who are quite prepared to take over the world. Do you know what those crazy dykes have done?"

"Excuse me, Ronny, I don't think that language is necessary here. I find it quite offensive."

"I'll tell you what those bitches have done. They have erected a statue of me that was actually carved from a great rock they quarried from the Chester Gorge and which Rhea must've given them when I was in prison. And they use it as target practice! Those bitches teach little kids to throw rocks at it while they chant man-hating slogans that the dykes have taught them."

"I'm afraid I must go, Ronny."

"There has already been violence. A youth found dead in the car park in Northampton, another up in Deerfield and a third drowned in the river at Shelburne Falls. And all of them Teightons. So all related to me. Call that coincidence? And how about this? That little bastard Leo and his mother know in advance about the murders and pass the news on to the old man—who of course accuses me of trying to kill off all the family so they don't inherit."

"Goodbye, Ronny."

"Smug bastard. You sound like a fucking relative!"

THE TORCH

Very soon after we had started chatting on the Internet I tried to visualize him. I didn't usually pursue this somewhat fruitless activity but his rather shy and modest allusions to himself made him peculiarly attractive.

"I might as well tell you right off the top that I'm a bit of a loser. I'm a cadet at the Burroughs Military Academy here in Troy, New York. Frankly, my grades aren't too hot, and I think I might flunk out. Only I'm not too bad with the computer stuff. That might save my bacon. But this is all so dull and boring. Tell me about yourself, Davey. What do you do?"

I've become pretty good at sliding over that one. I didn't have to hesitate before spreading it across the screen.

"Oh, I'm just a modern-day scribbler. Only I scribble for TV."

That seemed to satisfy him. At least he changed his line of questioning.

"Does your Mom sleep well at nights?"

I promptly decided to reply in kind. "No problem whatever—night or day. Then she's been dead for years."

He avoided that—at least he didn't slobber a lot of cliché condolences. Perry, as he called himself, turned instead to his own mother (as

I had anticipated by his question about mine that he would). " Mine is very much alive. Very much interested in my life. That's why I'm on the Internet right now. It's about the only time of the night or day I can assume she's in bed asleep and won't call me and ask what I'm doing."

I looked up at the big clocks I had Joe put up on my wall. They provided the time in various parts of the world at a quick glance. In the East it was three-thirty a.m., which meant not only was it half past midnight for me, but that I had been sitting there before my terminal for an hour and a half. I wriggled my backside. I would soon have to think about emulating Perry's Mom as I had a heavy day confronting me on the morrow. But that line of thinking was obliterated by Perry's next string of sentences across my dark screen.

"She blames me for her insomnia, and the nightmares about raging fires and infernos, which she says began with my birth and why she nicknamed me 'the torch.' That she claims has been responsible for all her subsequent visits to the funny farm she goes to on the Hudson River below Poughkeepsie.

"But that's just for starters. After hours of screaming that I'm to blame for all her unhappiness she suddenly changes her mood and says: 'Torch, it wasn't your fault what happened,' and asks me to forgive her. But years before all this, when I was just a little boy, my Dad (who was a state senator in Albany and so could fix things), had me taken away from her and my spiteful little sister Cassie, and sent to a farm in the Catskills. There I was raised by Dad's friend, Bryce Shepherd, and his family. My mom used to send me expensive or unusual gifts from time to time—as compensation, I always thought, for the fact she never visited me at the Shepherds' place. Mostly the presents, for birthdays or Christmas, were weird, like a flock of pedigree Southdown sheep. And last but by no means least she sent me a prize bull calf. I named the little fella Zeus because he stamped his hooves so proudly. I still have him even though he's long grown up. I love my fiery little bull and miss him a hell of a lot. As a matter of fact, while I'm away at college he's earning his living by taking part in the oxen weight-pulling competitions at the County Fairs. My ex-girlfriend, Iona, who handles him, has to explain to the judges that he is really a castrated ox—in spite of appearances to the contrary. Then she was always good at lying through her teeth and getting believed. No wonder she claims to have come from the gypsies.

"But back to that mad mother of mine. Her last gift to me when I was still in the Catskills was a bow and arrow which I looked forward to hunting with. Until I found the note inside the package informing me that she had covered both the bow string and the arrows with poison and that I was never to fire it as it could easily kill me. Sometimes I don't think that would be altogether a bad thing. I've got it here in my room, right now. It's all I've got as memento from those days. I could easily rig it up to go off and into me if I wanted."

"I don't think that would be a good thing, Perry. I think you should seek help if you feel like that. What about your friend Iona? Or where you are now? Surely there is someone you can confide in."

"Why do you think I use the Internet? Just because there isn't anybody. That I could trust, that is."

"But my dear boy—you don't mind my calling you that, do you? Only you are obviously a student and I am well into middle-age." (I left it there as I didn't feel old yet to this depressed youngster with his bizarre background, while if I admitted to being on the threshold of seventy, I could only appear as an old man.) "Well, here on the Internet you have absolutely no guarantee that the person you are talking to is BONE FIDE. I mean, there are some very weird people around and the electronic highway doesn't escape them, I assure you."

"That's all right, Davey. I know you can do me no harm way out there in Vancouver. Though I, too, have heard some of the horror stories. Women being badgered by men, lonely guys in dark basements talking hot sex to young girls, sex orgies being arranged. . . . Something new in the papers every day. It makes you sick."

"Well, Perry, we are patently free of anything like that. And God knows, you've been through enough—what with your Mom's mental problems and the uprooting as a kid. None of that could have been very easy. But now you can handle your own life. Once you get through school—and I do suggest you stick THAT out. I mean, an education, and that computer science you said you really liked. Only then do you need to decide whether you want to be in the regular army." I was running out of dumb comment and advice.

Perry's reaction appeared far more slowly than during the lengthy exposition about his past. "Davey, has it ever occurred to you that I myself may not be all that I seem? That my mother may not be the only one crazy in my family?"

That immediately brought my confidence to the surface. "You know, one thing I have learned over the years, Perry, even before the insights from the Internet, is that the more outsized a person's story the more likely it is to prove accurate. Pathological liars rarely go in for whoppers. They prefer to build up their fictions with small details—what my Cornish grandmother used to describe as using little stitches to make large embroideries. I knew you were telling the truth the moment you told me your mother had sent you a flock of sheep. People don't invent things like that."

"I also told you a little detail, too."

"And what was that, Perry?"

"I told you that my mother has always called me by her nickname of 'the torch.' She was right, you know. That is what I am. Over the years I have set light to restaurants, bookstores—anything that caught my fancy. I am an arsonist, Davey. Oh, too bad we don't have audio on the Internet yet. If we did you could hear what I am beginning to listen to as I type these words. It is a sound which I am very familiar with, and which you might not even recognize. It is the crackle of flames, the roar of fire. It is just beginning to grow louder and any moment now it will be partly drowned by the angry peal of the fire-alarms throughout the Academy. Yes, all three buildings I decided should go with me."

My imagination was vivid that night. I smelled the acrid smoke, began to hear the crackle of burning wood and the fall of masonry. I began to type on the wings of panic.

"Perry, get off the network. Pick up the phone and call the fire or police. Dial 911 or whatever it is there and tell them what's happened. For God's sake! There are other people . . . your fellow students. . . . You don't want to be a murderer—you must act at once. Please, Perry, believe an older man and do as I say."

I stopped. My heart was heaving, sweat burning my skin as I sat there in the cool of a Vancouver night imagining an inferno in Troy, New York.

I think I sobbed. If so, it was brief, for he was back there on the screen.

"Aha! Davey! You shouldn't believe all you read on your screen— even if you are old and think you know everything. Yes, I am the torch—that is my destiny. But not this stupid place. I wouldn't waste my talents on this shitty Academy. That's not the only reason though. There are other things I have to do. Other things have to happen. I want to see my Zeus again. And I haven't finished with Iona though I don't love her anymore. Oh, and so many other things of which you know nothing and will never know anything."

"One thing seems indubitably true, Perry. You may not be a complete liar—though what you've just done suggests a gross lack of proportion! But that apart, there is something remarkably wrong about you."

"Wrong about me? Ah, my friend—if you only knew the half! And like they say—the worst is yet to be."

SCORNED WOMEN

I have to admit that I am a slave to the Internet, making my obeisance dutifully each day and eagerly scooping up its offerings to both hug and puke over. But I would be less than honest if I were not to witness to some distinct shortcomings with the electronic highway. One of these is the lack of personal autograph appearing on the screen—even when the raw and intimate, the horrifying and grotesque, are being revealed by the words chugging implacably like a tiny freight train across the monitor.

So what was different, you might well ask, in *primordial* times when the typewriter was still in use? I'll tell you what. Even typewritten letters were authenticated with a signature, the minuscule shape of which could sometimes tell you more than the whole message above it! And this is something people of my generation learned early. By the time I was four, certainly before I was five and going to school, I had learned to make a sharp distinction between two longhand words: "Mummy" and "Daddy."

These names impinged most on birthdays when their invariable gifts of books arrived. Daddy's longish, close-together-and-hard-to-read name usually adorning the fly page of such as *Great Classical Legends For Little People*, or some such edifying, yet for me truly fascinating, tome. My mother's fatter, more rounded script, proclaiming her love for her little boy and assuring him he had a devoted *Mummy*, preceded less improving volumes such as Enid Blyton's *Sunshine Stories for Little Folk* or—following consultation with incipient natural historian me—animal or bird books about their young, with lots of drawings and exciting photographs of badger cubs, fledgling ravens, fox cubs and fawns—and tales of their successful rearing by knowledgeable humans when rescued from starvation as orphans when abandoned in the wild.

Those brief inscriptions and their accompanying personal icons became elevated into letters and even more tender endearments when I was long gone from parental care and living thousand upon thousand of miles from their Cornish valley and had settled in Vancouver. And now even those letters are stilled. Indeed, personal letters, let alone those couched in longhand, have become an extreme rarity in my life. Instead I experience the highly personal conveyed through the extravagant impersonality of the Internet.

As, for instance, with the communication from Boris Orfuss, an old schoolfriend who found me on the Internet by what he claimed was "sheer bloody coincidence."

I should say a few things about Boris—which means that I must say a few things, too, about myself. Very Brit is item one. We became lovers when both altos in the school choir at Probus School, and still having sex (although progressively spasmodic) when we were both attending university and both still singing together in the college choral society.

On graduation our ways separated, Boris becoming first a tenor with the BBC Chorus and then branching out as a soloist, embarking upon what looked like a most promising career as a concert artist. I went to France, met my life partner, followed him to his native California and—well, the rest is history, as they say.

I was reflecting on the divergence of our lives as he proceeded to throw his up on the screen. He mentioned various highlights of his career and also hinted at some kind of debacle which I inferred was connected with his wife, Stephanie, who had apparently discovered his having a clandestine affair with a young French medical student he had met when a soloist with an orchestra in Lyons.

I was thinking of how handsome he had been, from a choirboy, as an undergraduate and, from photos we exchanged, well on into his thirties. After that our correspondence had lapsed and I heard of Boris only through my mother who had initially been a friend of his long-deceased parents. After a recital in Plymouth he had rented a car and visited my mother and father at Polengarrow, our farm in the village of St. Kew. Mother had subsequently written me a long letter stressing his charm and incredible good looks for a man now in his forties. I reflected that I was thinking back when? Twenty? Damn!—nearly *thirty* years earlier.

Then I recalled something else. In a letter the previous winter my sole surviving brother casually remarked that he'd bumped into Boris in Harrod's and been saddened by how stout and totally bald my old friend had become. But I didn't think of the various corruptions of age—when you've reached my years you tend to skirt that one—but of an explanation of how Boris was writing his truncated biography before my eyes. Some "bloody coincidence" in finding me on the Internet! Brother Arthur and I e-mailed each other regularly. I knew damn well he would have parted quite happily with my electronic address. He was proud of how up-to-date we both were and would have been all too eager to share our prowess with a new convert to the medium.

My sight returned to the screen and my attention was suddenly quickened.

"So you can see, Davey, I really have to blame Stephanie and those bitches she calls her friends for destroying my career. Frankly, if it weren't for the boys, I would have left her ages ago. As it was I was blocked from any more work by that producer, Leona Thrace, after Stephanie told her I had the hots for her son. But did that satisfy our Stephanie? Not on your life. Next it was Semele Thrace on *The Daily*

Telegraph. I suppose you wouldn't know who she is. But her gossip column sells more copies of that revolting rag than anything else in it. You can imagine how I felt when I saw what she'd written: 'A certain well-known singer nurses a far from well-known appetite—for the children of his trusting and unsuspecting friends. This isn't a matter of 'Lock up your daughters' but your teenage sons.'

"No specific reference to me, of course, but a couple of obvious clues about a relation with a famous Greek restaurant in Soho and some Cornish connections centering on Penzance. That put paid to a Westcountry Tour twice the size and length of the one when I visited your parents. But even that didn't satisfy that bloodthirsty trio headed by my hate-filled wife. They then enlisted the help of my uncle's new wife—I refuse to call Eunice my aunt. She managed with one weekend of arduous telephoning to inform both sets of grandparents, my nieces and nephews, and even had the fucking gall to phone my boys and tell them to make sure they weren't ever alone with me. Fortunately the twins are loyal lads—and old enough to tell her she should be ashamed of herself. But you can imagine the shame I felt. I mean, when two fifteen-year-olds have to tell you not to cry and that they trust you implicitly—well, it doesn't do much for one's morale, I can assure you of that!"

I took advantage of an unexpected pause. "I guess hell DOES know more fury than a woman scorned? That is, a bunch of women scorned—or at least pissed off. But Boris, it's the '90s—surely your voice is long past—well, we're both a couple of elderly gents now, aren't we?"

There only came the bare words back on the screen, of course. But I could imagine the sullenness coloring them. "I was giving you the whole story. I didn't say all this happened yesterday."

But I wasn't going to be dismissed quite so facilely. "Nor last year, nor the year before, eh?"

"Wrong, my friend. It may have begun back then with Jean-Philippe writing so passionately to me from the Edouard Herriot Hospital in Lyons when she went through my mail. But I'm talking about now. Last January, you see, I took some time out. I don't have that number of voice students any more and they seem to pick and choose when they want to turn up for a lesson, especially after Christmas when they all seem to go off skiing or something. So when old Mrs. Langthorne offered to pay for me to have a brief winter vacation, I jumped at it. Anything to get away from all that hate, with those blasted women plotting behind my back that has become so much worse of late. The boys know there is something going on but they just try to ignore it. I suppose they just feel torn in two between us and it can't be very easy for them, poor darlings.

"So I went to Gozo. Lots of—well, shall we call them male couples—have places there. As a matter of fact I'd been invited to stay with my friends Ken and Larry who have a lovely apartment overlooking the Med facing Malta. To cut a quite complicated story short I met a new friend on my very second day. His name is Roberto but he calls himself Kelly. We fell totally in love—and you can imagine how truly wonderful that is for me at my age to have the love and trust of someone barely thirty. Kelly has relatives in London and since my winter holiday we have seen each other all the time. I would move out of here and share a place with him if I only had the money to afford it.

"Of course I told Kelly not to risk writing me as Stephanie and her cronies, who have almost moved in with her by the way, pounce on the mail as it slides through the letterbox before I can get anywhere near it. But I can hardly stop my darling from phoning. Not a day goes by—if we don't physically meet at his place in Islington—that he doesn't phone and pour out his love for me. He's a true Mediterranean boy, full of passion and longing. Then one day when we were talking—me in the low whisper I invariably use in this house—I heard breathing and knew that Stephanie was listening on the other phone. I didn't let on, but said something ineffectual to Kelly and we made our goodbyes.

My darling boy put his phone down when we had agreed to meet the next afternoon in Aberdeen Park where he is living with his uncle and aunt. I hung up, but then moments later picked up the receiver again. I heard a number being called and then Stephanie talking to her arch crony, Leona Thrace. She told her that she now had proof that there was another man—catamite was her term—in my life, and that she was determined to put a stop to it. Leona asked her what she had in mind and my heart almost stopped when I heard my wife calmly state that she thought an accident was in order, and indeed, had already discussed it with Eunice who has been staying here ever since my uncle passed away back in June! I can't tell you how careful I was to gently put the phone back in its cradle without that cow discovering she'd been overheard.

"Well, that's about it, Davey. I have been living in terror here ever since. I don't dare tell Kelly anything. He is far too hot-blooded and impetuous. I shudder to think what he might do in reprisal. As it is he keeps urging me to leave the place and go off somewhere with him. Apart from the twins—and Basil is still subject to those epileptic fits which seem to get worse rather than better, as the doctors had suggested would happen—I am virtually penniless. No students to speak of since I got back from Gozo. There are a few revolting recitals at community centers—how I hate singing to all those old crones who huddle in the lounge, knit and chat throughout my performance, and barely applaud when I'm through, but even they seem to be drying up."

I was just forming a sentence of elaborate commiseration and encouragement when he forestalled me.

"So the point is, old man, I'm at the end of my tether. I simply don't know which way to turn. Which is why I am wondering whether you might lend just a couple of hundred quid to tide me over. That could get me out of the house and Kelly thinks his uncle would employ me as a waiter at his place in Camden Passage. I told him that my own uncle had had the Greek place in Soho and stretched things a little bit by saying I had worked there for some time during my youth. In fact I used to help out occasionally when I was a student but that wasn't very often. But the situation at The Golden Fleece looks quite promising—if I can just make the first move and escape the clutches of these women. Of course, if you could make it a little more—shall we say for old time's sake? I would be eternally grateful."

I chalked up the moment as historic. This was the first time I had been hit for a loan on the Internet. The screen went inactive: he obviously waiting, me prevaricating as I mentally scampered for some kind of response. I was tempted to be bold and refuse him but boldness has never been my strong suit. As usual I compromised.

"I am not all that well off, Boris. But I will do my best. I will see a cheque is in the mail by morning. And now it must be goodnight as I'm dead tired," I added, quite truthfully.

The next morning I compromised on my offer: made out a cheque for one hundred dollars rather than pounds. Whether he was miffed at my miserliness I don't know. He never replied to my letter or attempted to find me on the Internet again. He did cash the check, though.

It wasn't quite the end of Boris in my life. Some months later I received an e-mail from my brother wishing me a happy birthday. But being Little Arthur he didn't stop there when there was still more space on the screen to be filled. "I don't know whether you heard," he added, "but your old friend Boris met with a gruesome end. He went skiing, apparently, to Kitsbühl, and had a terrible accident on the slopes. God knows how it happened but his wife and some of her friends found his body all twisted up in fantastic fashion—with somehow one of his skis jammed into his neck, almost cutting off his head. Not nice. But nevertheless, as his schoolboy pal, I thought you ought to know."

THEN AND NOW

THEN

"Hello, Davey. My name's Aris Sussfeld. You don't know me but I know quite a lot about you. I have seen several of the TV shows you've written scripts for. More than that, we actually met a couple of times. Once at Hamburger Mary's? Though that was some time ago. Then at the AIDS dinner last year when you were the guest speaker. I was the tall guy who stood up and asked you a question about the possibility of us AIDS helpers getting a hospice in Vancouver's West End? I was also the official photographer at that and lots of other social functions you've attended in the city. Another thing. Your friend, Nick Georgiadis, took part in the same photo exhibition with me at that wild gallery on Davie. Nick is a great guy. We had a lot of fun together. Through my many connections I've helped him get into several photo exhibitions around town including the male nude one that caused all the fuss which I'm sure you will remember. Nick is sure a good and loyal friend to you, Davey, which is something I think you ought to know in the light of what's happened."

My personal rule on the Internet was to keep things to relatively short statements, at least until some necessary information about each other was established and there was a mutual desire to continue. But this oddball had just sort of erupted and I hadn't got a single word in edgeways.

But that wasn't the all of it. I do have a friend named Nick, but he has spent the past eighteen months in the United Arab Emirates. And he's a mining engineer—and only a not-so-hot amateur photographer. If he had at any time come anywhere near having an exhibition, let alone selling a work, old blabbermouth Nick would've told me at once. Come to that, I couldn't for the life of me remember anyone standing up and mentioning the need for a hospice when I'd given that talk at the AIDS benefit.

But it would still have been hard to break the dizzying flow he zipped across my screen. Indeed, a few moments later his mood shifted significantly enough to persuade me to suppress my instincts as well as my self-imposed rules over Internet conduct, and let him continue, as my eyes widened with his words and I felt a distinct lowering of body heat and an involuntary desire to shiver.

" . . . But those aren't the reasons I've been trying to get you on the chat line, Davey. I've been wanting to tell you for a long time that you have—well, let's call them 'certain enemies.' People who would like to see you come to real harm. Now, I don't want to panic you—that's the reason I thought that taking the Internet route would be the best way. I could have tried e-mail but I didn't know whether you had an e-mail address. Fax, for that matter. There's the regular letter route, of course, but I wasn't sure how much time I've got to get through to you. And if you were thinking of the telephone—well, I was already pretty certain they have you bugged.

"What I'm talking about, Davey, is something I've heard. Heard in several places. Even in Little Sister's. You wouldn't think in a gay bookstore, would you? All very subtle, mind you. Lots of hints and the kind of underbreath remarks I pick up in my line of business."

I was about to ask him if he meant as a photographer but he anticipated me.

"You should also know that I do the odd criminal case. A private eye, that is. You know—a gumshoe? That takes me into some pretty odd places. Dark and smoky singles bars where you hear things. Now as I said, Davey, the last thing in the world I want to do is to alarm you. But these are the kind of people that mean business. Dirty business, that is."

I don't know where I found the willpower but I still refused to interrupt him. As his words persisted I glanced at the phone by the side of my monitor, and wondered at its possible treachery. But I quickly returned to the screen where the verbal picture he drew grew darker and darker.

"You may remember recently publishing a story on Socrates which centred on his trial, particularly emphasizing those charges associated with corrupting the youth of Athens. Well, I have to tell you that story has upset quite a lot of people, some of them very powerful figures even though they prefer to work behind the scenes. By certain guys you have been called a pedophile who is trying to use a Greek philosopher as an argument to help spread child-molesting and establish chicken rings around the West End. I have even heard stories of a book of addresses of pedophiles, and 'boy-brokers' who fix the prices and arrange the procuring of children to serve those seeking them for their sexual appetites.

"The fact you are a self-confessed gay doesn't help matters, I can assure you. And your modern-day defence of Socrates has made those who were cool to you beforehand much more angry. Not to mince matters, there are certain people who sincerely believe that child corruption should be a capital offense and that the Criminal Code should be changed to that effect. Now, as they don't for a moment think that will happen, a secret committee has been formed to ensure that all pedophiles are treated radically different from here on in. And

your name, Davey, it is my understanding, heads their list. I handle a
fair number of child custody cases—often where kidnapping is an
issue—and through this work I have been in touch with people who
frankly have lost all patience with the system and are quite prepared to
take things into their own hands.

"They have already started to do so but I don't think that specific
cases are public knowledge as yet. If the police know they aren't saying
so and I have seen nothing in the papers or on TV. But your story got
a lot of publicity and in some of the places my work takes me I have
heard everything from having you beaten up to torching your home
and even taking you some place and forcing you to take the same
hemlock brew that Socrates was forced to drink.

"That, unfortunately, isn't the end of it. You have also managed to
upset some others, too."

My willpower ran out. "I had no idea I was so famous. That anything
I've done or could do would be seen as important. I've only ever heard
of a couple of homophobic columnists who have written the odd snide
remark about me and my partner."

He more or less ignored that. "I am a messenger, a reporter. I don't
deserve hostility from anyone. Whether you know it or not you have
distinctly managed to stir up a lot of anger in certain circles. Anger
that's not going away and which I think you should be aware of. Hence
my contacting you in this way. You haven't endeared yourself with
some ethnic groups. I understand you have accused both Ukrainians
and Croatians of anti-Semitism. At least there are those in at least three
bars I could take you to who'd accuse you of slighting their ethnic and
religious backgrounds. Only they'd do more than just accuse you, my
friend. They take these things very seriously. So would you, I think, if
you were a Croatian, say, especially today with all the ethnic-cleansing
stuff being thrown around."

It was odd what his words were doing to me. Not for a moment was
I ashamed of remarks I might have made about the historic hatred of

the Jews in the Ukraine. And anyone with a smattering of World War Two history knew all about the Ustasi in the Nazi puppet state the Germans had created with an unhealthy compliance of too many of the citizenry in Zagreb and throughout Croatia.

Nor was I in the slightest abashed by whatever I had ever said or written in defence of Socrates—or against witch-hunts of pedophiles, or anyone else for that matter. At the end of the day witch-hunts and vigilante groups were more dangerous than a man in love with a pubescent youth. Of course small children needed protection and sadistic murderers and rapists were best behind bars. But I had myself seduced too many mature men when I was thirteen and beyond to be complacent about the contemporary distortion and obfuscation of language as to what constituted "a helpless child" and who was the victim when a teenaged boy and a man had had an erotic encounter, ten, twenty, even thirty years earlier. In fact, all these perfectly intact memories of those claiming they were corrupted or seduced in their childhood by the likes of priests and teachers made me want to vomit. If there was one thing we gays learned when discussing it was how faulty and often non-existent were the memories of those straight men with whom we'd had sex in our childhood. We recalled every minute detail while they had either suppressed or maybe just blithely forgotten what their hormones had led them to before encountering the female form.

But with all that said, I cannot say that the words and warnings of Aris Sussfeld did not leave me profoundly disturbed—more than that, strangely wracked with guilt. For how could I say that I had never used words that could racially hurt? That I had never said an unkind word about Jews? About the Chinese? About the parents I had been called to honor? No, it was not me who could afford to first cast a stone at anyone. This man pouring out his warnings and admonitions might be stark raving mad, be entirely motivated by his own sense of pompous self-importance. But what was any of that compared to being a hypocrite?

"Thank you for bothering to tell me all this," I wrote abruptly, quenching his flow. "I will take your warnings to heart and act more circumspectly. Is there anything else I should do?"

That of course, re-opened the floodgates, only the gear had shifted once again. "It took me some effort to tell you what I've learned. For one thing it could put me in jeopardy. You should also know, Davey Bryant, that I am an extremely busy man. The photography seems to have taken off and I am now wanted everywhere. I simply cannot keep up with the requests to show my work. And—I don't know if you are aware—but I totally refuse commissions—portraits, that kind of thing. It is my artistic output that is so much in demand. I am having to seriously think of cutting down my undercover work where I learned of these things I have now passed on to you. But I do realize I am fulfilling a public service and not a week goes by when some tearful parent is not on their knees thanking me. It makes me feel quite humble, I don't mind telling you.

"But it is not as if that describes the whole of my life. Jesus, no! I sit on so many boards—the symphony, the opera, the art gallery, the community centre on Denman. Then there's my local School Board—"

I was debating whether to just tell him to *stop*—or pray for Divine intervention—when he suddenly ceased reeling off his bloody list. He didn't stop writing, however.

"It has all just crept up on me in the past little while and I am now wishing each day had forty-eight hours. You can just imagine what a quandary I was put in when certain people started feeling me out to run for mayor. Of course I know I would be given secretaries and that. In any case I am already thinking of taking on some help as it is. But I don't want to burden you with my problems as it is quite obvious you have enough of your own—even if you don't face these enormous claims on time that I do. As a matter of fact I've often envied your kind of person—writers, that is—who can say something controversial in print like that child molesting stuff but still hold on to your privacy. Or could until these groups of concerned parents and the like got onto it. Well, I've told you all that. No need, I hope, to repeat myself. Before I go I might suggest you change your phone number to an unlisted one, or even move to another address—that would be even better for your safety, I should think. And frankly, Davey, I should get off that bandwagon about sex with kids and dragging in that Greek pedophile who committed suicide."

"Just for the record, Aris, that last sentence is simply a pile of shit. I have never stood for adult sex with truly immature and defenseless children. And as for Socrates—I place him on a level with Jesus Christ. Have since I was a child myself."

"I gotta go, pal. Sorry and that. But the phone's been ringing off the hook since midnight."

I didn't try and impede his departure from my monitor. After feeding on the solace of a blank screen I got up and helped myself to a couple of Tylenol. If I'd known that that wasn't the end of Aris Sussfeld in my life I might have finished the bottle.

N O W

If he'd given me his name right off the bat I might have just switched off the Internet. But he called himself Humphrey, babbled something about living common-law with a girl named Amy in a highrise opposite Lost Lagoon, and that they had a little girl named Harmony. He then quickly moved to another topic which inevitably grabbed my attention. He brought up AIDS.

"I'm on the Internet to you, Davey Bryant, because I know that among other AIDS organizations, you're in with the Hope House guys where people like me can go."

He paused for that to sink in, I think. He needn't have worried, though. It sank in, all right, dragging my heart down to my feet as it did so.

"I thought it would just stay HIV-positive. God knows, that was bad enough. I went around in a daze for months. I never told anyone. I was scared stiff, you see, it would get back to Amy. The day the doctor told me the lab results was the day before Harmony's seventh birthday. Don't ask me how I got through that day." He was silent again. I imagined he was crying.

"Then it sort of dulled. I didn't think that it had gone away—nothing like that. But I sort of got used to it. Then came the sweats. I could hardly hide them from Amy. That was when they put me on AZT. It's gotten worse from then on. The worst thing of all, though, has been explaining the KS lesions to Harmony when they first appeared on my face.

"I can't take any more. I never again want to hear Harmony explaining what she learned about AIDS in that goddamned school where they hear so much. Nor do I want to see Amy's expression when she doesn't think I can see her looking at me. I love them but I can't bear to be with them. It's just too much to handle when I'm feeling so weak and down. That's why I am talking to you now. I don't want money—that's not it. But I need help from someone who has influence with that place. And I remember you and the AIDS banquet."

Memory clicked. My fingers sped.

"You aren't Aris Sussfeld, from somewhere in the West End, are you? Didn't you talk to me a year or more ago?"

"Yes," he admitted. "Yes, I am Aris. Only last time wasn't—well, wasn't altogether true. Like I never mentioned my wife, or Harmony, did I? Of course you've got to remember I wasn't even sure I was HIV-positive then. I was still doing things—though I never told anyone. I guess I was more or less in denial, as they say. No one knew except whoever it was I met. That was always in the afternoons, of course. I mean, with Amy and that, when else could it be? I was never much of a photographer—though I did have a show at that place on Davie, near the Safeway where I work as a clerk. The other business—the detective work? Well, I'm afraid—"

"You don't have to tell me all this, you know. As a matter of fact I learned things that day about myself. And of course I'll do all I can over at Hope House—though I must warn you that accommodation is strictly limited. But I promise I'll do my very best. I don't have much clout but I can be persistent."

"That's all I ask. It's just that I'm at the end of my tether. I don't know how, after what happened the first time, I've got the nerve to call you on the Internet again. But I've really no options. I'm not a very important person and I don't need telling I've made a complete fuck-up of my life. Whatever is left of it."

"Please don't go on, Aris. You don't have to. I feel that somehow we're friends. We've been through things—glimpsed one another, that is. And I am the lucky one. I've played the same Russian roulette and for reasons I'll never know I can still go on saying the old cliché: " 'There but for the Grace of God go I.' "

"That was St. Paul who said that, wasn't it?"

"I don't know, Aris. That's to say I don't remember."

"My trouble is I remember too much. That's why I want in to Hope House so much. I'd rather remember alone."

"You'd better give me your phone number as well, Aris, so that I can quickly locate you if the Internet is down," I wrote, praying that this time he was telling the truth.

THE VOYAGE

Most of my life on the Internet is spent encountering strangers, but Jay and I corresponded by regular mail for years before we both discovered the electronic highway, almost simultaneously. The net result was to greatly increase the quantity of our communications and, rather oddly, to elicit from my old college friend an intimacy of emotion and candor of expression which his rather formal letters had invariably avoided.

It was in 1992 that he raised me on the Internet in an evident state of great excitement. He had decided to quit his job with the *Irish Times* in his native Dublin and emigrate to Seattle, where he already had the prospect of a job with a highly successful magazine his editor uncle Michael-Liam had offered him, as well as the required immigrant sponsorship which his mother's brother likewise promised.

I might add that Jay had never crossed the Atlantic, even though we had regularly invited him to visit us every time Ken and I were in Dublin, as *his* guest. But he had always found some excuse: He had a profound fear of flying; he couldn't afford it; his newspaper wouldn't let him go; his mother, with whom he lived along with his mentally retarded brother, was invariably unwell, with her arthritis or migraines acting up. . . . Excuses which became so lame over the ensuing years he made them that we were too embarrassed to persist with our tired old invitation.

How much his tune now changed. The Internet bubbled with his excited anticipation of being so close to us. Twice, thrice a week, the buoyant words danced gaily across my screen.

"I've already started packing things. There's a huge mountain at the foot of my bed! Seattle is so near you in Canada I guess I should start thinking particularly about winter clothing. What do you suggest? Woollies, of course. Long underwear? And will I need a heavy over-coat?"

We'd both told him so many times on our visits that the Northwest was relatively mild if damp in the winter months that I was tempted to be flippant but he gave me no time to suggest he come nude—by then he had already moved to the topic of transportation.

"I don't think I'm even going to have to fly, as I can get a Greek freighter to either Seattle or Vancouver. You know how I hate planes and this would mean I could actually handle the voyage as well as the exciting new life prospect awaiting me."

That was something else. Jay was capable of many things that could irritate me but I had never before found him pompous. "The exciting new life prospect awaiting me," indeed!

Nor did he stop there. "I'm going to get a Chevy convertible when I hit Seattle, Davey. I've been looking up maps. It's the I-5 between the two cities, isn't it? And I estimate I can get between your place and Uncle Michael-Liam's in just over three hours—maybe less. It takes me as long to get down to Cork from Dublin.

"I tell you, I can hardly wait to get out of Ireland. The place is sinking in apathy. No one has had a fresh idea around here since the death of William Butler Yeats!"

At that juncture I half expected a dissertation on Irish literary history, which in various versions Jay had delivered on prior occasions. Only in the past it has invariably been Ireland first last and centre—rather like gays boasting about Our Famous Heroes throughout history. Or, for that matter, we Canadians with our parlor game: Name American stars who in fact are Canadian. But now Jay was playing "I Hate Eire" and being very, very boring about it.

"Aren't you being a bit inconsistent, honey child?" (My favorite of the terms I knew he abhorred.) "I mean, you've been in love with Ireland at least since the first day I met you at Trinity College Dublin when we were freshmen. And you've always claimed to loathe travel whenever we've asked you to come and stay with us. And let's not stop there. I seem to remember you calling your now sainted Uncle Michael-Liam a stingy old fart who'd never sent either you or your brother so much as a Christmas card." I warmed to my task. "Furthermore, Jay darling, I certainly don't recall you ever expressing the slightest interest in even visiting this Pacific northwest, let alone moving here permanently. Come to that, how about your poor old Ma and her migraines and the total reliance on you by both her and your brother Aloysius?"

I knew that was below the belt, but that was what my relationship with Jay did to me. I was either loving him and thinking fondly of twenty years' acquaintanceship since our Trinity days—or he was speedily driving me mad and revealing whole tracts of my nature which I would rather have buried from my own sight—let alone his.

As we approached the end of summer and thus the approach of Jay's autumnal departure, his tone changed. Or perhaps *progressed* is a better way to put it. That's to say, his language grew even more grandiloquent.

"I shall be coming on the mighty wings of the equinox when the sun declares your fall—if—as a newcomer to your arcane American language—I am thus allowed to pun."

He wasn't getting away with that. "Come on, Jay! We took English together, remember? Have you forgotten that your own beloved Yeats wrote of autumn under The Falling of the Leaves?"

He airily brushed this aside. "You refer, of course, to 'the fall of the generic leaf.' Oh well, if you prefer the prosaic calendar—I will be there around September 22nd."

I think that was the last time I could've described what Jay wrote on the screen as "airy," for as the days were consumed and his arrival grew ever more imminent, paradoxically, his words became more tense and his mood more anxious. Jay has always been a bit of a worry-wart about minutiae—hence, I suspect, his previous antipathy to travel. But now I detected a much darker element mingling uneasily amidst his progressively strained attempts to sound jovial, or at least be his equivocal up-and-down self.

The trouble was the "ups" were no longer there. Now it was all anxiety manifesting itself in strings of questions. Questions that either I couldn't answer ("Do you think I'll get on with Uncle Michael-Liam's wife, Aunt Elley, whom I've never met?") or which were so trite I had no wish to ("Do you think I should buy a raincoat in Seattle or here in Dublin? Which would be cheaper?").

But that wasn't the worst of it, unfortunately. To start with, there was some fuck-up over the blasted ship he was taking from Cork. He wrote me screenload after screenload of anxiety-laced lament: that the *SS Argo* was to arrive much later than had been previously scheduled; that it would not be able to provide him with the specific outside cabin he had asked for and that instead of directly crossing the North Atlantic and following the coast south from Boston or New York, it would be sailing first to Brest in France and then directly to Panama and through the Canal before heading for Manzanillo, Mexico, and then up the Pacific coast, finally arriving in Seattle nearly a month later than had been originally stated.

"Well, I hope you've finally gotten your schedules worked out, Jay," I wrote. "Also that you are finally packed and that the problems with your aunt in Seattle are happily resolved."

"Do you know what? The route that damned ship's going to take will ensure the maximum time at sea. And that's something I know I shall loathe. Just because I'm terrified of flying cooped up in one of those jets doesn't make thoughts of all that ocean any more pleasant. I tell you, I *hate* the notion of miles and miles and day after day, of gray and choppy water. I am a land creature, Davey. It is only on terra firma that I feel at home.

"You ask about my luggage? Well, I've lost a suit, a jacket and God knows how many shoes. That brother of mine has been sneaking into my room whenever I've been out and helping himself. And if I say anything there's always Mother to scream at me about blaming her poor retarded child. I tell you, Aloysius may be an idiot but he's a fucking thief, too! Only she just doesn't want to hear it. Trouble is she cannot stand reality. Well, nor can I stand the atmosphere in this house—which is why I'm leaving. Why I'm prepared to risk all that horrid travel.

"And how do I know that I'm not going from the frying pan into the fire? You should've seen the last letter from that bitch who so clearly has my poor uncle under her thumb. Talk about putting out the welcome mat! She says quite brazenly that it is entirely Michael-Liam's idea that I come, and that she hopes I bring enough money to last until I'm making plenty. She also promises to make sure I don't sponge off them. And just in case I didn't get the full message of her out and out hostility towards me she adds a postscript about my having only a month with them before I'm slung out and go and get my own place to live. That is with me not having the slightest idea of the flat situation over there—apartments you call them, don't you? And don't forget, Davey, I don't have the slightest idea of how much a flat rents for.

"That bloody bitch is his second wife, you know. And of course it's now perfectly clear she's only married him for his money. I suppose the whole thing boils down to the fact that I simply can't take any more of this frying pan home and will just have to pay the price of my fears of sailing and the uncertainties awaiting me in Seattle. That is landing in the uncertain but bound-to-be-hellishly-hot FIRE!"

He stopped—I presumed to hear some words of consolation from me. I was certainly relieved that a heavy heart doesn't show up on monitors as I slouched forward on my swivel stool and addressed the task of cheering him up.

But first I made a big decision. "You know that if things don't pan out for any reason, Jay, you can always stay here with us." I hadn't finished typing those words out before I started to compose a persuasive announcement to proffer my roommate, at that very moment sleeping innocently, unaware of what possible complications I was about to risk introducing into our lives.

"But you mustn't paint too dark a picture of the future. I know you, Jay. I know just how black you can see things when you're in a certain mood. In your case it isn't so much a matter of not counting your chickens before they hatch but of not assuming there are any chicks to start with! For all you know you may well have mislaid the odd garment or article rather than Aloysius having taken it, the ocean may be cobalt blue without a wave in sight and the trip will pass more swiftly than you dare imagine. And as for old Aunt Elley—well, she might turn out to be okay after all. I mean, Jay, that construct is as good as another. Just don't be so bloody negative for a change. See the old pint mug as half full of Guinness rather than half empty!"

I paused, not out of flagging invention but to see how he was taking my homespun therapy. In the end he produced the equivalent of grudging agreement.

"You might have a point. I certainly hope you have. But somehow, for better or for worse, I feel I am already on a train, a ship, a plane—it doesn't matter—and whether I like it or not, I can't get off. So this is it, Boy-o. I go down to Cork tomorrow and wait for the Argo to arrive from Liverpool. I've already e-mailed Uncle Michael-Liam and told him to expect me whenever the bloody boat decides to make it to Bremerton which, incidentally, I gather is the port for Seattle, though God knows how far away.

"I'll send you a postcard whenever we call in some place—and it looks like we won't be missing a single port after Panama. At least you might like the stamps! And Davey, thanks for the invitation. And thank Ken too, will you? I'm really grateful and it takes a lot of pressure off of me over the possibility of things going wrong with my relatives or at the new job."

I was still thinking of a suitable reply when, by the sheer lapse of time, it occurred to me he'd already quit the Internet. For him by then it was mid-morning. Knowing what a procrastinator Jay was, I hazarded he still had one hell of a lot to do before making those tearful goodbyes to both his elderly mother and squint-eyed Aloysius and then taking the train south.

But it didn't end there. Not by a long shot. First came the promised postcards. Then one day in early October, not the expected phone call—but would you believe it—a bloody e-mail from Seattle. It was, of course, you-know-who informing me that Michael-Liam (the first time Jay had ever skipped the "uncle" designation) was a computer buff, replete with all the PC paraphernalia from fax modem, e-mail, and on the Internet, too.

That wasn't all he told me. Not by a long chalk.

There was first a truly terrible story. It explained his puzzling silence since arriving in Washington State after the regular arrivals of all those postcards.

"At the start everything went splendidly, Davey. They picked me up in Bremerton and took me to their truly lovely home in Issaquah. It is tucked right in an evergreen forest and there were marvelous flying squirrels right outside my bedroom window. I have a whole wing to myself. And Aunt Elley has turned out to be a real brick. You were quite right over her, you see. And the job situation has also turned out to be tops. If only I could continue in that vein. But I can't. Oh Jesus-Mary, I can't!"

I knew silence was what was required from me. I just waited.

"It was on the weekend. I had hardly got my unpacking done. In fact that has something to do with it. I had bought a brand new pair of slippers, fur-lined moccasins, in that posh shoe shop in Gresham Street. Well, somehow, one of them had gone missing.

"More as a joke than anything else, really, I came out of my room just wearing the one that was left. I explained to Aunt Elley who saw the funny side at once. She directed me to the deck off the living room where Michael-Liam was doing something with a planter. I just stood there in the entrance, where the plate glass windows were pulled wide open. There was no time to say anything. I'm sure he looked down at my feet and saw the one slippered foot and only a white sock on the other. But he didn't smile. Didn't say anything. Oh Davey, he couldn't—there wasn't time. At that very moment he must have leaned back on the balustrade of the verandah—and it didn't support him. One moment he was standing there with a trowel in his hand. The next he was gone. Gone down the almost precipitous slope at the edge of the trees which led to the river below. God, it was awful! All so horribly sudden—and so final. Aunt Elley screamed and then there was just silence.

"He was dead when we found him, Davey. His head smashed against a rock. Can you think of a more dreadful, pointless accident?"

I could not, of course. But it took time to absorb his shocking news.

"Are you still there?" he asked.

That jerked me into renewed activity. "Of course," I typed. "It must have been quite terrible for you. For his wife, too. Now, Jay, I hope you aren't taking it all to heart. Blaming yourself, that is. It was obviously just one of those ghastly accidents for which no one's to blame. How is his widow taking it?"

"She's spent a lot of time sobbing in my arms. I just stand there holding her as she shakes and shakes. But she's quieter now. We just sit about and she tells me over and over how great Michael-Liam was—what a marvelous marriage they had for those seven years. The magazine has been very good. My uncle's second-in-command is now acting editor. He has told me to stay with Aunt Elley for just as long as it's necessary."

"Would you like to get away for a spell? We'd be only too happy to have you, you know that." I had an afterthought. "Your aunt, too, of course. Perhaps you could both do with a change of scenery."

"I think for the moment, Davey, we should just stay put. The funeral was only six days ago and there's still business stuff here in the house with which I can help her. But it's awfully nice of you to ask. And I would like to take you up on it one of these days, okay? In the meantime we've got the Internet and that's an enormous help as I've been able to talk to loads of his friends and business acquaintances. I just couldn't use the telephone—I just can't talk about it with people I don't know while I don't mind communicating with them this way. I guess I'm very odd or something."

I wasn't going to dispute that but then was not the time to tell him so. "Well, just call me up whenever you feel like it. I'm usually on around midnight—that is, after Ken's hit the sack."

It was several weeks before Jay finally brought up the question of a visit. I remember the date very well—American Thanksgiving. His aunt had told him she wanted to see none of her relatives so soon after her loss and that giving thanks was not in her current vocabulary. It was then he'd suggested a trip to Vancouver and she had sounded most willing to get out of town and even visit another country.

"She's originally from San Francisco and that's where they always went for their vacations. She's only been to Vancouver a couple of times but she liked it very much. Says it's a really beautiful city with a marvelous mountain backdrop. Now, are you sure it won't be inconvenient? We could easily stay in a nearby hotel and see you guys each day, you know."

"Just like we could've stayed in the Gresham in Dublin and not at 43 Drogheda Road with you people? Bullshit! You are staying here and that's that."

I had one more Internet conversation with Jay before they arrived.

"Greetings, Davey!" Jay wrote. "The closest thing to good news for far too long. When Elley and I come to Vancouver I shall have an assignment. From CASCADIA REVIEW, my employer that Michael-Liam founded. They want an article on freighter travel for tourists based on my own experience getting here. Now as luck would have it, the old Argo will be coming into Vancouver from Alaska just in time for our visit! And if that wasn't enough, I've discovered an old fellow who lives on the Sunshine Coast which I gather is within easy reach of your city. This chap is a world authority on freighter travel for private passengers. He's sailed around the globe everywhere and has even published a book on it called SLOWBOAT TO ANYWHERE. He's agreed to an interview and I know that Captain Zetes and the First Mate, Peter Tiphys, will really put themselves out for me. So apart from the break and the sheer pleasure of seeing my oldest friend again, I will be paid for the pleasure and get all expenses thrown in. I couldn't ask for more than that, could I?"

Their arrival, indeed the first two days of their visit, was utter delight. Elley turned out to be a dark, vivacious woman, who obviously adored her nephew and kept up a quick flow of talk with him as if she could not bear him to be silent now that her man would never talk to her again.

The Sunday was brisk and cloudless. A harsh blue sky hosted an anemic sun and the wind blew in from the sea. When Jay put the phone down it was to announce that the Argo was in port and his friends in the crew were ready to meet him that very morning. In fact it was the best time, they told him, as Monday they'd be loading. There was a couple, a retired army colonel and his wife, whom Jay might find particularly useful for his article. Jay then suggested that we might all enjoy an expedition to the docks on the north shore where the ship was berthed.

The idea appealed to both Ken and me. We decided to take our car and combine the jaunt with a trip around Stanley Park and show our visitors some of the charms of the city which we hadn't yet taken in.

In the light of what was to happen I am glad we did that: glad that we drove slowly under creaking elms with the top down, listening to the stiff breeze fluttering obstinate brown leaves and sending bright white spume off the agitated waves. Some people, a lot of women, do not like the wind. But I have always loved gales, the roaring angry tempests that rage our coast and crescendo the empty beaches and send gulls wheeling crazily into a storm-cleansed sky. I think . . . I hope that Jay liked that scene too.

I don't know what I was expecting of the *Argo* but it certainly wasn't the rusty hulk lying there in the stagnant calm of the basin. We were just up the gangway and walking towards Captain Zetes who stood there with outstretched arms when it happened. From overhead where the crane was suspended, it fell. Not part of the crane but a bit of the flaking superstructure of the decrepit vessel. Aunt Elley screamed but it was on Jay that it fell. Striking him down in weird synch with Captain Zetes' arms falling back to his portly sides.

What else is there to tell? What else is there to know? Only that that piece of the *Argo*'s outworn structure falling on my friend so sadly, so sourly, completes my story.

ORVILLE

"Hi out there, Davey Bryant! They say to know all is to forgive all. I don't believe that. Want to discuss it? Have you got the time and patience? Otherwise I'll skip Canada and try some place else." Thus did Orville from San Francisco introduce himself.

I don't think I would have taken him up had I not that day completed eight days jury duty over a skid-row killing of a Greek sailor involving a drunken young Native woman who had smashed his skull in with a broken beer bottle. Lots of gore, drugs and whoring, lots of bitter swearing by a teenaged unwed mother of two apparently neglected children.

And in response, lots of condemnation in the jury room. But lots of sad social history too: a life of sordid rooms in transient hotels, of despair and a battered body that endlessly harvested purple bruises and foul-smelling, supperating cuts with the advent of every rusty freighter arriving in dock.

I told Orville I would be happy to share the Internet screen with him.

"Where to begin? With what they think is the worse thing about me? Or what I can't forgive myself for?"

I would have shrugged if it would have shown up on the screen. "The choice is yours. I'm just all ears—I guess I should say EYES."

"Trouble is I don't know whether you're like them or me."

"Nor will you unless you try me."

"The SAN FRANCISCO EXAMINER called me 'The Mom Murderer,' The CHRONICLE simply said 'Market Street Matricide.' It adds up to the same. You'd better know right off that I was responsible for my mother's death. I am not apologizing. She murdered my Dad when he was taking his bath in the Palace Hotel—and not content with that she then killed his girlfriend. Mine was only revenge, if you see what I mean. I don't care what anyone says, she was an evil woman and I vowed to kill her when I grew up. And did."

"But you're still alive."

"I was arrested, tried and freed—split jury. But there was still a whole bunch of women who pursued me whenever they could and screamed at me for what I did. I think I would have gone mad if it hadn't been for one person—my lover, Phil. We've been together for thirty years. I've seen him grow from a teenager with jet black hair and smooth skin to a white-haired man with a bunch of scars from a few motorbike spills as a California highway patrolman who still makes my life worth living. He makes up for the years I was forced to stay in Baja California when that horrible bunch insisted I was mad, kept calling me and saying they wanted to drink my blood after slitting my throat and then tossing me into the Bay.

"When I came back with dear Phil we both thought it was to start a new life. And at first it seemed that way. It really did."

Instinct prompted me. "Tell me about that, Orville. Tell me about the good times." I knew that there were other times, darker moments he was dying to relate which would surely follow.

"We bought a little house out on the Avenues, in the Sunset district towards the ocean. Actually a cul-de-sac called Angus Street. It wasn't very fancy. Just a small white two-storey—like all the rest on the block. But we loved it. We loved the sheer anonymity of it. If you had only known the publicity from just being my parents' son, let alone the homicide and the trial and all the hate that had stemmed from that—you'd have appreciated what the sheer sameness and quiet of those streets leading out towards the ocean meant. It was the closest thing to heaven that Phil and I have ever experienced. We had a grand piano in the tiny living room, which was already stuffed with furniture we had put in storage during our 'exile' in Mexico.

"And this is something I've never told anyone up to now. My Phil used to like to dress up. You know what I mean? We didn't discuss it much. But there were just nights when he got home from his patrol work and we'd have supper and then he'd go into the bedroom. I didn't need any more clues. I'd go right to the piano stool and take out some sheet music. Classic Broadway musicals was what he liked. The oldies like PAL JOEY and OKLAHOMA!, and especially OKAY from the twenties. Phil was very fussy about his entry number. It had to be something really flashy, with lots of syncopation that I could thump out as he entered the room. He always came out from behind the avocado we had grown from a pit into a big bushy plant. And what an entrance it was! A gorgeous red wig, a swirling green boa and a sparkling sheath of green lamé over sweet little silver slings. And, of course, the long white gloves and royal handbag. The whole bit.

"And a funny thing, Davey. Phil was so proud of that outfit and the rest of his gowns and stuff—yet he never wore any of it except in that room and except for my own two adoring eyes. No one ever saw my Phil in drag except me. And you are the very first person I've ever told, pal—believe me!"

By this time I was wondering why, in fact, he was telling me. He didn't leave me in suspense for long.

"I guess you've noticed I've been using the past tense. Well, here's why. Our happiness—after all the misery and murder that lay behind us—wasn't confined to that little house where we could live such private lives and play whatever games we liked. We also enjoyed walking, especially out by the ocean and the undulating dunes and the wind-twisted tamarisk. We were both men of action, you see. Both of us had been soldiers in Korea when we were drafted. So often, especially on weekends when Phil had the time off, we would walk for miles out there, from Fleishacker Zoo to the south, beyond Ocean Beach, right up to the Cliff House and the view of the seal lions barking out there on Seal Rocks. We knew all the quiet paths where we would be unobserved. We used to tell each other that when we reached such and such a big clump of sea grass on a sand hillock we would stop for a rest. But that wasn't the real reason. The real reason was we wanted to do out there in the briny air, under that huge vault of sky, what we so often did on the softness of a mattress in the gloom of our shuttered bedroom.

"I'm not talking of sex. Or rather, not only sex. But the feeding on each other's love that had grown so intensely and so steadily over the years. Sentimental? Romantic? You bet your life! We were both conscious that what we had was so much better than the crude sex we'd known when we'd fallen in love with the various high school kids who almost worshipped us when we were smart OTC cadets at Stanford.

"I'm not denying there wasn't something beautiful about that. I know it's despised now and people are flung in jail if they as much as look at a beautiful boy. But those kids back then taught us to be proud of being young men and would-be warriors. At the same time I think they learned some valuable lessons about courage and loyalty from the likes of us.

"But I'm getting off the point, aren't I? As Phil and I lay in the soft sand of the dunes with the roar of the Pacific in our ears, we actually welcomed the mutual grey in our hair, the hoar frost on arms and thighs. Even more, as we gazed into each other's eyes we saw exactly what we now shared. I had taken on Phil's gentleness, his incredible loyalty, he adopted my refusal to break, to give in when it looked as if the whole world wanted to bring me crashing down. I like to think, Dave, that Phil and I are something of pioneers as older gay lovers. By the Gods—we're more in love now than when we met over thirty years ago!

"But I'm still keeping off the point. What's the word? Prevaricating, I think Phil calls it. It's not something I like to dwell on as I think you'll appreciate when I tell you. It was just like I've described to you. There we were this blustery Sunday morning. November 9, if you're the type who likes details. I recall blackheaded gulls, crying and wheeling, as Phil and I lay down in the lee of a particularly steep dune which years earlier we had nicknamed the Acropolis for some reason now forgotten. It was somewhat closer to the ocean's edge than many of the hills of grassy sand dunes that stretched as far as the eye could see and was usually reached from walking along the shore as it was much more difficult to trudge through the soft silver sand from above and behind.

"We lay there, loosely entwined—Phil beneath me—both of us smiling in the exhilaration of sunshine and the smell of salt brought inland on the wings of the wind, and we talked our happiness. There were no clouds. When the shadows did come it was from the tide-glistening foreshore and not from the sky.

"Before either of us saw anything tangible we grew mutually aware of an alien presence.

"'I think there are lots of eyes fastening on us,' Phil said suddenly.

"With difficulty I turned my head towards the huge breakers but could see nothing else. 'It must be the gulls,' I said. 'That's why they keep swooping over us. Gulls are always crying sadly. They're not used to happiness like ours.'

"As usual, my lover was less blithe. 'It's not gulls I can hear. There's a hissing out there. And it isn't the wind in the grasses. There's a sound like serpents but I don't think it's snakes. Certainly not rattlers out here. Too cold, for one thing.'

"I listened too. Sure enough there was a strange noise that seeped through the vigorous breeze and was quite apart from the whispering

fronds of grass. It was a humming, that is, a subdued kind of singing—
the likes of which stirred my memory but which I couldn't pinpoint at
that moment. I decided though, that it was soft and high enough to
come only from female throats. Then physical shape was added to the
eerily persistent sound as the strangest apparition appeared around the
bluff of the dune, blocking part of the ocean from our sight.

"Even as we disentangled and sat upright, a trio of weirdly clad
women wearing grotesque masks under locks of unkempt hair danced
like dervishes as they advanced towards us, the ugly humming through
the tight slits of their masks sounding ever louder. If it was a chant they
were making, it was surely a diabolical one.

"No matter the masks, their flimsy tunics seemingly fashioned in
another age. It was at that precise moment I knew who they were. I was
back at the hysterical outbreaks during my trial, for Mother's murder.
Back at the street confrontations on Market Street before Phil and I
could escape into the family suite at the Palace Hotel, back twenty years
just prior to our flight to Mexico.

"I remembered those three veiled hags who had screamed and yelled
their hatred of us both as murderous fags. Someone told me they were
called Trish, Meg, and Alice, but they didn't deserve the dignity of
human names. Phil always called them the Harpies. I thought he was
just being dismissive of them as troublemakers—until, that is, we met
up with them again there amid those lonely goddamn dunes.

"I know it sounds a bit of a cliché if I say that from there on in
everything happened so quickly. But it did, it really did. I'm not
referring to how speedily Phil and I got to our feet, searched around
for something to defend ourselves. Because, make no mistake, those
three swirling bitches meant business. As they came closer and closer I
felt my Swiss army knife in my pants pocket and withdrew it. I glanced
at my lover and saw a similar red object in his hand. We had given one
another the knives after breaking up an attempted mugging on the way
home after leaving a performance of ELEKTRA at the Opera House.

" 'We'll take one each,' Phil said softly. 'I'll take the thing on the left.'

"I guess he figured that if we took two of them out the remaining one would present no problem for the two of us. Phil was always good at thinking on his feet. A hard grin crossed his face. I remembered not only his love of the thrill of battle but his fierce urging me on when my will began to falter over dealing with Mother in those last, horrible moments.

"Then no more thoughts, no more distractions as we braced ourselves at the very moment the Harpies came screaming toward us, their skinny hands raised claw-like to find our faces. They knew no fear.

"I had forgotten how physically trim my Phil still was from his weekly workouts at the police gym. Or perhaps I was surprised at the rock-like hardness of our assailants, at least the one I had elected to bring down. From the corner of my eye I saw my lover's arm with the now-opened knife at its end, reach through the swirling, dirt-stained dress of the creature before him, but before I was aware of whether he had reached its flesh my arm was knocked down, a squirming body was pressed against mine and fetid breath blew unpleasantly across my face.

"Her talons clawed my face, and I realized that it was not my cheeks they sought to gash but to find and gouge my eyes. That was when my chivalrous hesitancy over possible gender was banished and I knew our combat was mortal. These three must have observed us over many weekends to be so certain where we would probably be and thus consummate their venomous will.

"My knife pressed against scaly skin and suddenly sunk up to its shaft. Only then did the remorseless humming stop. The body, surprisingly light if brittle hard, rested across my arms. Then, a final revelation. As I held the creature up, turning the torso to extract my knife, her filmy skirt drifted upwards to reveal her legs. They were covered in scales, like those of some monstrous bird, right down to the feet which were but coarser versions of the claws that stood in lieu of hands. That whole portion of her anatomy reminded me of nothing so much as the giant thighs and legs of an ostrich or emu. With horrified disbelief I looked at my lover. He, too, was holding the lifeless form of his attacker, only he was holding it up high and twisting it around in the manner of a victor proclaiming his trophy.

"I think we were both surprised at the shriek which turned to a shrill and sustained scream as the third assailant shook talons frustratedly at us both before turning away from the confines of the niche between the dunes and ran madly back in the direction from which they had first appeared.

"Things went balletic. At least, it was all done in silence. With neither looking at the other we carried our lifeless charges down to the roar of the water's edge. I took one last look at my corpse; thought inanely along the lines of the parlor game—was it animal? It certainly wasn't vegetable or mineral.

"I decided that my would-be avenger was 'Alice.' I spoke to Phil for the first time since we had vanquished his harpy. 'I think mine is Alice. What's yours? Trish or Meg?'

" 'I think I've killed Trish.' He sounded so matter-of-fact—as if he were simply about to dump the garbage. He might just as well have called her 'Trash.'

"He read my thoughts. We often do so nowadays. 'We'll give this TRASH to the ocean. The fishes can eat 'em. Or maybe the sea lions—the big bulls will think they're found some kind of sodden bird. Those bastards are always hungry.'

"I grimaced. 'Not if sea lions have any taste. God, she's ugly. I think they're some kind of mistake. They'd have vanished from the earth years ago but survived on a diet of hate. Here, evil old bitch! Let the waves take you.'

"As her scaly skin slid roughly across my hands I shuddered. I wasn't minded to remove the mask. She disappeared in a frenzy of foam as the last breaker dragged her tumbling in its frothing wake.

" 'I don't think so,' Phil said, still holding the shrivelled shape of his 'Trish' in his arms. I swallowed hard when I noticed that he hadn't bothered to remove his knife from her ribs. I wanted to remind him but couldn't summon the words.

" 'If you ask me,' he said slowly, 'these things were meant. Right from the very beginning. They had no more say in being here than we did killing 'em. Here baby, join your sister.' With that he flung his burden to where mine had finally disappeared.

" 'You can tell that to the cops,' I said. 'I ask you, do your fellow patrolmen sit around talking about fate or destiny?'

" 'I only know one thing right now, Orville. We gotta go again. You realize we just can't stay.'

"The sun still shone in its fall frailty as if nothing had ever happened. But it had of course. We had silenced forever two of the Harpies. I think we both guessed the third no longer mattered. It was only in their plurality they'd counted.

" 'What you are saying is that we must again go into exile. That's the price of what we've done, Phil. That or another trial is something I couldn't stand.'

" 'That's what I am saying, loverboy.' He cupped his hands. Hollered out towards the invisible horizon of the heaving ocean. 'Hello, Mexico! Here we come!'

"I shook my head. 'I'm sick of the past repeating itself. That's what those two were all about. The same thing over and over again. I haven't the strength anymore.'

" 'What about us?' Phil said. 'I've got enough for the both of us, baby.'

"We clasped our bloody hands over the spray, and for a moment I didn't know whether it was Phil's words that blurred my sight or the salt from the sea.

" 'During Vietnam,' I said slowly, 'some of the bravest went north to Canada.'

" 'Okay. Canada, then.'

" 'It isn't that easy.'

" 'It never is, Orville.'

"That took longer than I thought it would, Davey. It was Davey, right? I guess you're a good listener. That is, if you're still there!"

For what seemed the first time in an eternity I typed in a contribution. "Yes, I'm still here, Orville. That's quite a story you had to tell."

"Well, it isn't quite over. We're back in the house now but I'm sure there'll soon be enquiries. Phil thinks so, too. In fact this was his idea. Any chance of us coming up there to you in Vancouver? Wouldn't be for long, of course. We'd soon get our own place. At least think about it. I mean it would be harboring known criminals and all that. There could be a murder rap at the end of it for us. 'Accessory After' stuff for you."

Impossible, of course. The risks were immense. I didn't think for a moment that Ken would agree. But the weirdest thing happened. I started off intending to say that I didn't think the Internet was the best place to make vital, life-informing decisions, that . . . that . . .

"Of course," I wrote. "We would be delighted to put the two of you up. Do you have some kind of date?"

"Real soon," came the reply. "I'll be in touch in a day or so. Around this time of night, you said it was your favorite time—right?"

But that was eight months ago. There is still only silence from San Francisco.

HID ON AN ISLAND DRESSED AS A GIRL

I think my first mistake with Achille Peleron was to accept the idea that we were both bonded by the sea. It began in one of my early on-line conversations with my new French-Canadian acquaintance which centred on our common marine pasts.

I should also add that it is a local story. That is, local for me. I very much wish it were not. It is one thing to learn the bleaker and bloodier aspects of someone living thousands of miles away—quite another to find that bitter grief, burning anger, and a terrible temper are as close as your own backyard.

I exaggerate slightly. Achille, though born in the small Québec town of Gethsémani on the north shore of the St. Lawrence, was living on Galiano, one of the islands offshore from the British Columbia Mainland where I live, when we first encountered each other on the electronic highway. He had hardly told me this before he revealed he was a sailor. At least, he *said* that he was a sailor. All I can be certain of is that he appeared to be as wedded to a sense of the sea as was I—a Cornish fisherman's son who had deserted family tradition for life on solid soil.

Achille's motives for leaving the Canadian Navy and his life as a naval officer were very different from mine. But that was something I learned only slowly. Very slowly. The first of our late-night conversations was taken up with far different matters.

One of them was the subject of our mothers. I think I was feeling more expansive than usual that night. There was a full moon and I could see its silver spill across the waters of English Bay. But my lover, Ken, always pooh-poohs suggestions that such things influence one's behavior. In any event I told Achille that I felt very much the inheritor of my mother's genetic structures. I think I went even so far as to describe myself as a prisoner of Mama's genes—at least in comparison with the lesser sense I felt my father inhabited me from the grave.

Achille was positively enthusiastic in his agreement. He claimed his love of the sea came purely from his mother, herself the daughter and granddaughter of mariners. However, he did not say it with pride exactly; rather, I think, to stress the inferiority of his landlubber father who also had the misfortune to come from a distinctly lower social stratum. I don't think I need add that Achille was a snob.

In fact his references to his father, Pellin Peleron, were scant and it was obvious that his mother, Thérèse, had been—perhaps still was—a dominant force in Achille's life.

"Maman could tell you every fish in the St. Lawrence. She taught me all about the smelt, sturgeon, and herring as well as the gentle beluga whales, and the walruses which were abundant when she was a girl. She knew every species of sea bird and the great southern migrations each fall. She never tired of telling me about the snow geese that nested on the tidal marshes at Cap-Tourmente."

"I guess like me," I interrupted, "you had to learn a whole lot more names of birds and animals as well as plants and flowers when you moved out here to the west coast."

But I think he was now bored with natural history. "And a whole lot more, my friend. I had to learn how to keep a low profile, to avoid the police and take on a new identity. My life has not been easy since the dreadful times I had to escape."

I was tempted to let him expound his cryptic remarks without help from me. But I was feeling generous. Maybe something to do with the lateness of the hour, as it was nearly two in the morning. Or it might just have been connected with my liking to play the primarily passive partner with these Internet conversations, as for so much of the rest of my day's activities it was markedly otherwise.

"Dreadful times?" I echoed. "What were they then?"

He was more oblique than my patience would have liked. "It's hard to explain to a stranger how much a friend can mean to you, especially when you're young and vulnerable and surrounded by enemies. My friend's name was Patrice and we went to the Collège Militaire Royal at St. Jean together as cadets. We were more than just friends, Davey. We were more like brothers. Bloodbrothers, as the Germans say. And how he liked sailing. Day after day in fact, whenever we could take time off from our studies—both there in St. Jean and when we were later transferred to the military college in Esquimalt, when we could sail in the Straits of Juan de Fuca. Boy did we have fun! Have you ever been out there between the Olympic Peninsula and Victoria, Davey? Jesus, the wind can blow! Not that we minded how rough it was. Patrice's folks were nautical types, too. It can be pretty rough in the mouth of the St. Lawrence, you know.

"Lots of the guys would drive west to Sooke and then head up the west coast of the Island through the rain forest with the moss and those huge banana colored slugs that went double their length when they were coupling. But not Patrice and me. We were happiest with the brine in our hair, the wind stinging our cheeks and watering our eyes as we rode the swells and looked for orcas. Old Patrice became quite an expert on those killer whales. Knew where their pods were, could tell one from another by the nicks in their tailfins, and would point out to me when there was a cow with her calf in tow. He was a bit like my mother then. I'd tell him so and he'd laugh and look embarrassed and tell me to shove it. But it was true, you know. He was a lot like Maman with his love of nature. And if the truth be told, his love of me, too."

I stirred. So at last we were to get to the nitty-gritty. But luckily I didn't hold my breath. "Jeez, Davey. Look at the time! Remind me when we are up on the network next time to tell you about that bastard Hector. The guy responsible for all my troubles. He was tied up with the killer whales out there at the mouth of Puget Sound. It all connects. You'll see. That is, if you want to hear all that. If you don't just let me know right now and we'll call it quits. I'm not the kind of guy who bends back ears just to be listened to. I got the impression we might have even more in common than our love of the sea, that's all."

I couldn't for the life of me explain his abrupt change of mood. But then was patently not the time to pursue it. I took the most conciliatory tone possible. "Of course you don't bore me, Achille. I'd have been gone from your screen long ago if I had been. Just check me out around midnight here and you'll probably hit pay dirt. And then we can explore our pasts if you like. My hunch is that we have more in common than the sound of the sea."

He didn't respond and it was a second or two before I realized he'd already departed from the Internet for the night.

The next time—which was a couple of days later—his gambit was quite different. In fact he spent the whole session yakking about how much he hated the Canadian criminal justice system, though without being the slightest bit specific. It was on our subsequent session, the very next night that he confessed to murder.

It started somewhat more innocuously.

"Do you believe in horoscopes?" he asked.

I had decided to be a little bit less supine this time around. "I think they're crap. In fact it depresses me that newspapers still print them, knowing that there are still sufficient suckers to take in all that simplistic nonsense. It robs people of the power to act for themselves—let alone being a denial of free will. We are what we make of ourselves and that's what makes everything worthwhile."

I was still thinking of further strictures against that and other superstitions when he started to write again.

"We're not going to agree on this one, Davey. It's like we grew up in two different worlds. You and I might share a love of the sea but before I even heard of the tides from my beloved Maman, Papa had taught me words like 'kismet'—made sure I knew what my fate was to be. I grew up from childhood knowing my destiny. My father was more concerned to let me know I had bad karma than anything else. I always cried when he told me what my fate would be but that didn't make any difference."

I bit my lip. I wanted, of course, to ask him what that fate was but my nerve failed me. Instead I wrote: "Horoscopes aren't exactly the same thing, are they? I don't think they have anything to do with our destinies. At least I hope so, they are so banal. In any case, they are invariably wrong!"

"My Dad didn't tell me that next Wednesday would be a good day for us Pisces. He just told me over and over again that I would die in agony as a young man and that at the time I would be living on an island, hiding from the world."

My mind raced to reassure him. "Esquimalt, where you were previously was on Vancouver Island. So Galiano is just a smaller one, right? The same could be said for the Ile de Montréal, or Manhattan. Nearly sixty million Brits live on an island, for that matter. I shouldn't worry about it. In any case, Achille, you don't strike me as a coward, let alone someone afraid of his own shadow."

This got to him. Struck a chord. "I may have changed my name and no one here knows who I am—can't even have a clue! But before things happened, before my life was destroyed, I had a whole squadron of ships. The youngest Commanding Officer in the Service. No, I wasn't known as a coward, Davey. Nor did my superiors think so. Not in the

Middle East in '73, or again in the Persian Gulf when I had my last command and was again honored—just before I had to disappear, as it turned out."

"You were proud of your naval career, weren't you? And of course you had every right to be. Especially for one so young."

"Not everyone said that," he replied. "I had enemies long before that bastard Hector took away my friend. But they were insignificant gnats. Just jealous of me—and maybe of Patrice too."

"You haven't told me much about Hector," I observed.

"I did not wish to. One does not readily bring up the name of the person one hates more than anyone else in the world. I loathed him before he killed my friend. I still loathe him now that he is dead, nicely bruised and battered before he bled to death at the end of the rope I tied to the rear bumper of the car. Unfortunately, I could not hear him screaming as I roared up the Malahat Highway with him in tow—and that I still regret to this day."

"Such hate!" I wrote hastily. "Such a thirsty vengeance! You must not let it destroy you—and those things so easily can."

He was dismissive of my sermonizing. "I am already destroyed. I was destroyed the second that evil bastard killed my Patrice. The rest is farce."

I was taken aback. I could think of nothing remotely comic about what he had written on my monitor that night. It also made me think yet again what manner of man I was conversing with.

I tried something else, not for the first time cursing the mask of the screen which demanded a constant reading between the lines to find the flesh of emotion, the colors of motivation that lay beyond his words.

"So this Hector murdered your beloved friend and then you killed him. Doesn't that equal the score? Aren't you now free to start all over again?"

Don't think for a moment that I believed my own words. But that is what had to be said. That is how the world runs—mine, that is, not Achille's.

"There is no freedom in any of this. The Gods gave me Patrice and they used Hector to take him away. My slaying of Hector was inevitable. It is all ordered, all a pattern—even though we can see most of it only in hindsight. That is why death is a revelation, my friend, which I shall surely soon know."

I couldn't stand his wooden passivity. If he were right in all this then I was an arrogant fool playing let's-pretend games about accomplishment and ambition. I thought of my Ken lying sleeping beyond my study wall. Was he just some inescapable factor in my life whose love I had never had to earn nor he mine?

I breathed heavily with frustration. The philosophy I was receiving from Achille was perhaps fit for sun-crazed people living on a pittance, off arid land—or all those hapless captives of poverty who were utterly contingent upon the uncertain kindness of strangers and the quirks of weather and brute circumstance.

But I had no chance to deliver myself of such sentiments, to point out that *we* strove to live by the creed of *noblesse oblige* because my lover and I considered we had so vigorously mined the motherlode of life we had a duty to put something back into the kitty.

"Before I die there are other things I must suffer. I have left these to the last because they cause me most shame and the world's scorn. You might laugh when I tell you."

"Whatever else, Achille, we have come too far in these sessions for me to laugh at anything connected with you."

"For a start, I should tell you I'm not known here as Achille."

"What's in a name? As Shakespeare asks in ROMEO AND JULIET, 'that which we call a rose by any other name would smell as sweet.' "

I'd no sooner gotten the words out than I cursed my pedantry. I wished it were sensitive Ken who was awake and sitting there in front of my computer and that it was I lying innocently asleep and thus incapable of making such stupid remarks to such a distressed voice appearing as plain words on a diminutive screen.

I need not have bothered with the self-recrimination, however. Achille was in a full spate of candor. "In this place my name is Phyllis."

I staggered from pedantry to plain stupidity. "But Phyllis is a girl's name!"

I am convinced Achille was as emotionally deadpan at that moment as his words suggested. "It is not only a girl's name but here I wear women's clothes. I arrived as such and no one on the island knows me as other than Phyllis or has seen me dressed as anything except a girl."

"We have a good friend here, a young architect who loves drag. Looks marvelous in it, come to that." I paused. "Are you a transvestite, then?"

There had been clues earlier in his temper, his penchant to feel slighted, but what now came forth dwarfed any previous hints that this was a wildly passionate man for whom grief, tragedy, and the humiliation of being hunted, had honed into a human Vesuvius ever prone to erupt.

"I thought I had found a sympathetic earhole, but what I have found is an asshole! Do you really think I am some kind of skittery drag queen fit for your gay bars and cabarets? Do you believe you are corresponding with some tortured transsexual who is dying to have his balls cut off and his tits enlarged—is that what you think?

"Well, I may be Phyllis here, of the blonde wig and the slim body who wears a tartan skirt as I stroll the beach, and a close-cut sheath when I entertain the handful of friends who first came here with me when the police started to close in. But I am also he who has slain dozens of the enemy and never taken prisoners. Ask any who have served under me and have seen me rage in the heat of battle exactly what I am capable of. Yes, I can wear a girl's garb, walk as a woman, made love with my Patrice as a woman. But only an idiot would take me for the stupid male generalization of what a female is supposed to be. I—who slit

Hector's throat from ear to ear before towing him into hamburger meat—am no transvestite, no transsexual. But don't think I haven't heard the taunts. I know what they say over there at the naval base. 'What name does Achille have now that he has gone away to some island and hidden himself among the girls there?' is the malicious quip of my enemies in the officer's mess at Esquimalt.

"Over them maybe I am powerless; I must endure their spite, put up with their scorn. But not from you, who are just some stupid diversion for me as I sit here, suffering the hours until death closes in."

Then even this worm turned. "Even so, Achille—or Phyllis, if you now prefer—I have been content to read your confessions and all your ill-temper which has colored your life and brought you to this terrible pass. I may not be the best of listeners but I can assure you I am far from being the worst."

He changed his tune with characteristic abruptness. "The mistake was wholly mine. My friends beseeched me to stay away from the Internet. I know it isn't private and is roamed by brainless motormouths. That sooner or later my enemies will catch up on me from it. I also know that you, Davey Bryant, will never understand the likes of me—where I'm coming from—what makes me tick. Then why the hell should you? I was wrong to expect it just because we had the sea in common."

I didn't respond. There was nothing profitable to say. But he had at least persuaded me that his death was truly imminent. For that dubious reason I left the initiative for him to proclaim his departure from the screen. Considering the imbalance of his life and mine it was surely the least I could do. I was even glad I'd quenched my curiosity and never discovered his actual age—though I would dearly have liked to know.

THE BEAUTIFUL BARMAN OF BANFF

"I was swept off my feet when I was sixteen by a man who said he had the finest hotel in the Rockies and promised to train me to run the bar which he said had a magnificent plate-glass window overlooking the mountainside. He also promised me my own stables with my own stallion and mares when he learned I was crazy about horses."

Later I was to meet him in the flesh, but it all began on the Internet with an extraordinary statement by this young man I shall call Troy Smith.

"I knew all right what he wanted when he threw me that certain look that guys do but that didn't bother me. Anything was better than life in the East Kootenays, where my Dad beat up on me after hearing some of the kids at our high school in Creston screaming 'cocksucker' at me. He was the principal, you see.

"After the night he kept kicking me in the head when he got me on the bathroom floor, I told myself that was it—and remembered meeting Zed a week earlier in the car park at the New Troy Restaurant on the other side of town. He gave me an invitation to visit, plus his card with the eagle feather in the corner. That was after I'd gone down on him behind Al McKay's old Chevy truck, which was all that Al got to use now that his young wife, Debbie, had run off with their Olds and that Pete Ares from grade twelve—who I always thought was queer like me.

"I didn't see my dad next morning at breakfast, though he must have smelled the French toast all over the house as I burned one slice of it waiting to serve him. He couldn't have known my ear had stopped bleeding, of course, or that I had stuck three jumbo-sized Band-Aids over it and the side of my head before combing over it from the back with part of my ponytail.

"Maybe he was ashamed to see me that morning. Like when Mom had died two years earlier he had cried for days on end because he felt guilty at not calling the ambulance in time.

"The idea came to me when at classbreak we were all out there in the playground, most of them down by the willows in the shade while I was keeping out of their way in case they started on about the Band-Aids and calling me a fairy again. I don't know what it was that made me look up but it changed my life, I swear to Almighty God and every Gideon you can lay your hands on.

"Way up there were three eagles circling. Parents and their young-sters, I decided. Around and around they went, higher and higher as they searched the thermals. I sighed till I was empty. How I envied them! How I longed to be an eagle more than anything in the world. I heard one of the doors in the toilets slam. It wasn't too far away from where I was standing. That decided me—or maybe there were lots of little decisions all in a row. Anyway, I didn't wait to see who it was but slipped out of the school grounds and back into our house next door. I ran up to my room. Not that I expected to see anyone. Dad was at school, of course, and our cleaning lady had the day off. I grabbed my dollar fold I kept in the covers of my bird-guide and hightailed it to the Greyhound depot on Main Street."

There came his first pause after signing on and responding to my urgent request for a chat when he had so baldly claimed he was the most beautiful barman in the whole of the Rockies.

"I hope you believe what I am saying," he now wrote. "There is no need for me to lie, you know."

As ever a slave to curiosity, I assured him I believed him implicitly—adding that in my experience people rarely boasted about their good looks unless they actually possessed them. That certainly seemed to satisfy him, for he was immediately off again.

"Zed—that's my friend—the one I was telling you about? He gave me this computer and stuff for my last birthday. That was only two months ago—on June 29—and I can pretty well hack it. Not bad, eh? Mind you, that Zed is a crafty one. As I figure it, he thought I was spending too much time outside—what with the horses and the barn I fixed up for what I call my eagle hospital. I've been caring for them and a few other birds for a couple of years now. People now bring them in for me to care for. You'd be surprised. Broken wings, bits of wire caught in their talons so they're starving. Then that goddamned DDT gets into their food chain. Even up here in what they like to call the unspoiled wilderness!

"Where was I? Oh, yes—Zed, being crafty and that. By giving me the computer and the modem he sees a whole lot more of me. He just likes to sit in a corner and watch what I'm up to. Of course he could see me at nights when I'm working the bar. But that's different. I'm too distracted then, reading the orders and mixing the drinks. It's different down here, though. This is the special room for the two of us. People have to get permission to come in here.

"This is where things happen when Zed gets all excited over me. We have different bedrooms upstairs in the hotel. He explained things right at the start when I came here to live. A hotel is like a goldfish bowl. There aren't too many secrets that go unnoticed, I can tell you! Zed thinks people don't know about him and me but that's bullshit—if you'll excuse my French. There's more known about what he gets up to than he dreams of—but it doesn't matter. Most of them are scared shitless of him, anyway! After all, he's the boss, the kingpin. What old

Zed says goes, I don't mind telling you. That committee of his he's always consulting are just hangers-on.

"Not that he doesn't get up to his own bits of hanky-panky and thinks I don't know it. But I do. I wouldn't be saying some of this to you right now if he wasn't up at the School of Fine Arts going to some French movie they're showing there. But I know my lover's got sex on the brain. Nothing, but nothing will ever satisfy that one! Boys AND girls, mind you. No one can ever put too many labels on our Zed. Not that I'm not his favorite, even though I say it myself. And I can also say that he is the best sex this boy's ever had. And even stuck away up here I could have more or less what I want. My looks have sort of given me a reputation here in the Banff/Lake Louise area. Even further than that, for all I know. Well, I do know. I have had people come in the bar where I mix the drinks for Charley the bartender from as far south as Cardston, where the Canadian Mormons come from, asking for little old me.

"They haven't even seen pictures. Just word of mouth as it were. Though there have been photos in the Calgary Herald since I started the eagle hospital. But they sure don't come here looking for me to get their wings mended or even their feathers smoothed. Know what I mean? Say, what did you say your name was?"

"I'm Davey," I replied. "And I'm in Vancouver—and if I wouldn't describe myself as looking like Dracula I wouldn't say I'm more than just run-of-the-mill either."

"That's all right, Dave. You'd be surprised. I don't go just for good looks. If I wanted that I could always look in a mirror and change my name to Narcissus or something. No, I like people with MINDS. That's what Zed's got. But here at Banff it's mostly slim pickings for the old gray matter. Zed encourages me to take courses at the School of Fine Arts but it isn't easy. I prefer using CD-ROMs home here.

"Fact is, I never have stopped learning since I got off the train from Creston and found him waiting as he promised on the platform. He had already signed me up for literature and film courses and got me into hotel admin before the first week was out. There's also the art appreciation I take in Banff, too. I tell you, twenty-four hours in a day's too short for me, Dave. Like I told Zed—if you keep me going at this rate there isn't going to be time for all the sex you want. In any case I'll be too tired to suck your cock, for one thing. He got THAT message okay. When it comes to rationing his sex-life with yours truly, he can react fast enough!

"Not that I'm grumbling, Dave. I certainly don't want you to think that. When I start adding up what I got when compared to the average guy of nineteen—that's what I am now, by the way—then I'm one of the real lucky bastards. This is what I got. Mind if I jot them down? Makes me feel kind of good."

I was about to give my assent but Troy had already assumed it. I don't think I've ever encountered anyone so spontaneous on my monitor. Then I suppose I was already beginning to fall a little in love with him.

"First there's Zed, of course. He's the greatest. After all, I wouldn't be sitting here talking to you if it weren't for him, would I? Then there's my job. You know I always wanted to serve the public somehow. They say that barmen get to know some of the deepest secrets of the human race. And I'm really a sort of barman. I mix the drinks, you see, when they come in. My very favorite thing is when we have a banquet for the Rotary and I get to pour the Pouilly Fuissé that Zed gets specially for us from the winery he owns in Sonoma, California. I get to use the goblets of real gold that came from the old Palace Hotel in San Francisco. Zed got them at auction.

"I haven't even mentioned my string of horses, have I? If you could see my sorrel mare and my golden palomino stallion you'd just water at the mouth, Dave. When I tell you they are just beautiful, it's like I'm understating. I have the finest horses in the world, Zed says. And he should know. He knows more about horses than anyone. He even sent two down to Creston to that asshole father of mine who kept calling me a cocksucking faggot after the scandal at school when he first thought he'd lost his job. Then Zed is generous like that. I won't even talk to the s.o.b. Not that he ever calls. Got a new girlfriend, I figure.

"And this year alone I have tossed three golden eagles and one bald eagle up into the air from my barn steps and watched them fly up into the sun. I tell you there's no feeling like watching those big buggers sailing—after you've nursed them back to health from being all bedraggled, skinny, and with their wings so often broken and hanging till I put them in splints. I tell you I cry when they soar up there into the blue. Eagles flying is a kind of poetry I believe. And do you know what? I keep one single feather from each of my babies. And when I have nursed enough of them well I'm going to have a cape made from those single feathers. I know a cute Indian guy, Brad, who helps out on the ranch, who has promised to give me a hand. He's a western Cree and knows all about feathers.

"Then the fact that the Almighty dealt me a full flush when it came to my features is just another reason to go down on my knees. Not for what you're thinking, Dave—you dirty old man!

"Not a bad list, is it, for someone who hasn't seen twenty yet. By the way, for that birthday Zed is going to take me down to Vancouver. Perhaps you and I can meet then. Though on second thought I guess we might be a bit busy with sightseeing and that. I guess it wouldn't be the best idea—not right on my birthday, that is. I don't know how long Zed intends to stay, see."

But he had planted a mad seed in my brain and it stirred immediately.

"I want to finish a book I've been working on and already have a grant to come to Banff to do it," I wrote. "I'd been thinking of coming the end of this September or the beginning of October. Maybe we could meet then, if you like."

"I like," he typed back. I was glad he couldn't see me slump with relief, nor feel my pulse beat and a faint sweat moisten my palms as lust swiftly flicked acrosss my body.

So much for the electronic introduction. I have to go to my journal now—a very far cry as it is written in old fashioned long-hand—to give you the rest of the story. It is dated November 1, All Saints Day. I could make no record of the following for several weeks after my return home to the loving care of my partner Ken.

I flew to Calgary and took the bus into Banff. By late afternoon I was sitting in my rustic cabin designed by a nationally-known architect, as were all the others scattered about the forest paths and affording quiet and concentration in the depths of the woods for those of us writers, painters, and the like who could use them as workplaces during the day.

The one I had been rather grudgingly allocated boasted a grand piano, as it was intended for a composing musician. But by its charm of design, the fact it was even more remote than its companions, as well as the unexpected opportunity to play what music I could remember from a singularly distant past had me pleading to occupy it daily, between breakfast and supper during my time at Banff.

But as I explored its nooks and crannies, and thrilled to the sight of huge and silent-moving elk wandering in and out of the thickets on every side, and the hopping of inquisitive magpies curious to check out the new tenant, and the shrill chatter of fractious squirrels, my thoughts had nothing to do with these delights of nature nor to the book I was there in the wooded mountain valley to complete.

Outweighing both natural diversions and stern duty was my antic-ipation of meeting Troy. The arrangements we had made a week earlier, on our last Internet session, were simple enough. I was to go to the bar of the Eagle View Resort Hotel that evening and inquire for him.

But in the event that trip proved unnecessary. With my laptop unpacked, a few provisions tucked away in the waiting cupboards and yet further marveling at the enormous height of the bull elk whom I'd been warned at the main building were still in rut, I was sitting strumming a few bars of Schubert's *Impromptus* when a heavenly sight swung into view down the snaking and sloping path. Coming towards me was a young man who, by his sheer beauty, I was convinced was Troy.

The vision of loveliness saw me at the same moment I first fed on him. A smile spread like a soft flame across his features and made him even more radiant if such were possible. Had he been in the cottage with me I would have had to greet him in silence. My throat was dry, my lungs devoid of air, so great was my joy and appreciation that he had come to search me out rather than wait for me to seek him.

The grand piano was at the furthest point from the front door of the studio room. There were a couple of chintz-covered armchairs and a small work table between the piano stool and the door and I bumped into all three as I sped over the one or two throw rugs to anticipate the knock. As I tore the door open his hand was just going up. Unlike mine, his voice was in full working order. "So you must be Davey. I recognized you coming down the path but not from the description you gave me on the Internet. You were far too modest. I am _____."

He gave me his real name which I will not disclose. Finally the words came. "This is a wonderful surprise," I croaked. "Come on in."

But he seemed as impetuous in the flesh as on the Internet. In fact he gently brushed me aside and by the time I'd shut the door and turned to face him he had taken off his windbreaker, unwound a pale blue cashmere scarf, and thrown them on one of the armchairs.

"Don't ask me why," he said, through the most perfect teeth I have ever beheld, "but I just knew you'd be in the composer cabin. It's my favorite of all of them, though I do like the painter's one just two up the hill from you."

"So you know the whole set-up. I had no idea."

But he seemed intent on his own path of thought. "I told Zed you were coming today. You are to have dinner with us at the resort. He'll send the Jag. But don't dress up. It will be quite informal. We have guests who come down to dinner the first night as if they are on some ocean liner. But by the second day they dress as casual as the rest of us."

I was appraising his own sartorial wear that very moment: a cashmere sweater, a darker shade of blue than the scarf, covered a creamy, open-necked shirt. Below a silver-buckled cowboy belt were plum-colored cords and what they enclosed in their uppermost frontal parts threatened to once more take my breath away. I swallowed hard and forced out a welcoming "Sit wherever suits you most, my dear." (And felt like an old queen as I said it.)

But once more he seemed not to notice my words as he had already flung himself on the small sofa by the Pullman kitchen and beckoned me to squeeze on it with him. Celtic caution and thirty years of covert sexual dalliance combined in me at that moment. I glanced quickly at the cabin's three windows in turn. Noted which had a path beyond them down from which we could be seen and also registered with mild frustration that there were no drapes that could be pulled to screen us from sight.

However, where my Adonis had elected to drape himself was certainly the most protected spot from unwonted eyes throughout the cabin and dismissing my already waning caution I sat gingerly, indeed rather primly, at his side on the few inches left that his slender body afforded.

I felt things must be slowed down somewhat. "You seem to know your way very well about these cabins in the wood," I said. "I won't ask you when you last visited this one."

He was searching my lips hungrily. I thought I would faint. My knuckles were about an eighth of an inch from his fly. I could feel the body heat emanate from him.

"Visited this one," he said slowly, cocking his head slightly as he did so. It was the first time my sight had travelled beyond the clear blue eyes, the delicate arch of his brows to the nacreous neatness of his perfect ears. I was about to devour them mentally, too, when I noticed the tiny ivory object inserted there.

I willed myself not to raise my voice one iota. "You are just as beautiful as you said. More so if possible."

He smiled. "The forest is very beautiful. You have seen the elk herd. They're everywhere this year. But I'm afraid there are no possums."

A little cloud began to unfurl in the dim recesses of my mind. I gave it a nudge. Fully aware of the watch observable on my wrist I looked down at his bulging crotch as I inquired softly, "Do you have the time?"

There was a slight pause, wholly unlike anything I had read from him on the Internet screen, where he had been my fastest correspondent by far.

"You want to have sex with me, Davey? Zed says it will be all right. He is not jealous—provided it does not interfere with his needs."

The realization that something here was amiss wouldn't go away. I willed my hand not to move a millimeter closer to him, however much its fingers longed to travel.

"You did not hear what I said, did you?" I smiled into his eyes as I said that, as if I were really asking him whether he liked walking in the silent woods with the elk and the squirrels as company.

He smiled as gently back at me, and pursed his lips in invitation. I fiercely willed the endurance of that phony smile. "The truth is, darling, that you are deaf, isn't it?"

"Darling," he said, his own grin broadening with the triumph of lip-reading, "I'm Zed's darling but there is enough over for you, Davey. It was our fate to meet on the Internet. Our destiny, our karma."

Now it was my turn not to hear *his* pathetic words. For that matter I could no longer see him through the scrim of tears. My excuse for finally crushing him to me, enjoining our lips and tongues and the lengths of our bodies, was that I would not have him see my distress.

But that was short-lived. I could not proceed into the territory of sexual passion without committing one disruptive action. Roughly, I broke away, produced the balled-up list of instructions from the Banff School of Fine Arts which I had casually stuffed into my trouser pocket. I took out my ballpoint and as he quietly watched, I wrote out the terse question:

YOUR DEAFNESS. WERE YOU LIKE THAT WHEN WE SPOKE ON THE INTERNET?

He nodded, and spoke before I was through. "It was what my Dad did. I told you. But it doesn't make any difference. Zed says that it is our imperfections that make us more beautiful than ever. The things in each other that we fall in love with."

Only then did I think I noted a slight slur in his diction. As if there was a minuscule pause in his brain between the formed concept and its articulation. And with that awareness I joined him again, thrusting hard, hard against his suppliant shape. But my flesh sought solace rather than sex.

ADIEU, ARTEMIS

I was going to call Artemis on the Internet and tell her something about him but I was ignoring her feminine intuition and her singular ability to size me up. She was having nothing of my compassion for his deafness acting like the opposite of an aphrodisiac.

When I provided her with a tentative and much-laundered account of the sequence of the events that first day in the cabin at Banff, she sent up a flurry of letters and images on the monitor which I took to be her Internet equivalent of a skeptical snort. She then resorted to more coherent communication.

"You've got to watch it, Davey. We've reached that age when we can too easily go overboard. I hear women say that their troubles will be over with their last period and that menopause is spelled 'marvelous.' They know nothing about it, of course. Or they wouldn't talk so silly."

I had never heard my old friend refer to menstruation before. I wasn't sure it was a seemly topic between a middle-aged matron and a middle-aged gay. That didn't seem to be her attitude, though.

"I'm glad we can talk, darling, in this way. You know there are certain subjects that should only be addressed by two people, and only on the Internet. This is one of them."

I was about to point out that I didn't know as yet precisely what the subject was but she again forestalled me.

"I won't say too much about faithfulness in terms of either you and Ken or this child tucked away in the Rocky Mountains with his extraordinary sugar daddy. That's because you're a man and invariably silly over disciplining the loins."

I wasn't going to let even beloved Artemis get away with that. "Silliness seems to be your theme-song this evening—but don't forget you were using it of women only a minute ago. Now it's us men. Does that let only you off the hook, then?"

Again she took a dive into rarely swum waters. "It's just one of those areas where you gays merge with all the other kind of men. In other respects, darling, I am quite prepared to acknowledge the difference. There are those bits of you which you share with us women and then, of course, the other bit which is SUI GENERIS and thus not transferable to the main genders."

"Thank you so much for the enlightenment. Now I won't have to take Biology 101," was all I could muster—uncomfortably aware that as riposte to her it was very sub-standard. She seemed, however, to be in a generous, if excessively analytical mood. That's to say she ignored me.

"I do worry about you when you go away on these trips, you know. You are so prone to romantic excess. It's your heart I'm concerned over far more than that of dear Ken. He is altogether more rooted and with an infinitely greater sense of proportion. Now tell me more about that man Zed you mentioned. He's the one that fascinates me."

"You just called him a sugar daddy!"

"And since when has that been a term of abuse? You are confusing it with 'gold-digger,' dearheart. And I don't think even your magnificent mute was really one of those from the way you describe him. But let us continue with the mysterious Mr. Zed. What an intriguing chap he sounds!"

"I haven't really told you all that much about him—save that he has patently been so kind to Troy and acted most pleasantly to me."

"By sharing his boyfriend, you mean. Yes, well, I was thinking along rather different lines. Didn't I gather he is a man of infinite wealth and diverse appetites? Also that he visits Vancouver from time to time?"

"I did say those things. But your reiterating them sounds suspiciously mercenary, my dear. Although I'm sure, of course, that is not your intention."

Whether she was mollified or not I never found out for she simply changed the subject. "In the welter of detail I cannot recall whether you gave his age or nationality. Though you did mention property in California and a penchant for horses like the lad."

"Greek, of very good family, I believe. His father was a Kronny, I understand, and his mother one of the famous Rhea sisters. Then the gossip is that he is a first cousin of King Constantine II and with a primary claim to the throne, should the country ever go royalist again."

"And obviously as rich as Croesus."

"Obviously. But more successful with his various projects."

"He sounds very accustomed to authority."

"Many executive types are. Especially Greek CEOs."

"Now you are being grudging, Davey. I don't really deserve Who's Who answers to my questions."

I relented. I knew my Artemis well enough to fill in the pout behind the emotionally anonymous words before me. "He told me one night—when Troy was pouring him what I thought were unusually generous libations of his favorite Pouilly Fuissé, that he owned the world's largest hotel chain with its headquarters the famous Olympus Palace where he was in fact born—in its pre-hotel state, of course.

"A bit of gossip I got from Troy—Zed was at one time married to his own sister, who is in fact the nominal president of the hotel chain, even if they are no longer on speaking terms. That's all a bit mysterious."

Artemis broke in at that point. "Incest among the Greek royals is hardly your usual cup of tea, is it?"

I was not about to be deflected by her social observations. "Then there's his connection with the armaments industry. I gather he is a major shareholder of WeatherGod Inc., which came up with the new thunderbolt missiles. 'A man with broad interests,' as Troy loves to put it, 'that cover land and sky, day and night.' "

There was an uncharacteristic pause from Artemis. "I have the oddest notion I am related to Zed," she finally responded. "Only it is all little tufts of dream that float in and drift out again. Like those bits of cloud one zips through when coming down to land at an airport.

"There are certain things. . . . Do you recall my telling you I was something of a hunter when I was a teenager in the Basilicata? Well, if I think of my childhood in Italy, for some strange reason your Zed comes to mind. A tall, commanding figure forever barking orders. I have a vague memory of being swept up in a warm male scent, warm male body hair. I am almost suffocated. It is isn't quite frightening, and not quite erotic. But related to each. And the thrill of the hunt and the sense of soaring at great speed through the sky—like an eagle. Those are the kinds of thing going through my head, even as I write these words for you to read."

"Zed is tall; immense in every sense as a matter of fact. And he's certainly authoritative. Not bossy, mind. But a man of enormous assumptions."

I didn't venture further at that point. I was intrigued by what I was learning about Artemis herself. Once or twice she'd vaguely mentioned youthful time spent in Italy. But not the Basilicata. And I certainly had been ignorant of her exploits on the hunting field. Relentlessly pursuing bargains, yes, but darting from shop to shop wasn't the same as galloping from field to field. Nor could I reconcile a white sales trophy with some lifeless furry thing dripping with blood. It was all very odd, as she herself had said.

"It sounds very odd indeed, Arty. Do you have anything else to go on than these vague impressions? Something you have suppressed, maybe?"

"I don't think so. But there is something else. I know a nutty woman on Bowen Island. She constantly harangues me about her pet peeves, of which she has more than holes in a colander. The chief of these is her fear and loathing of males and she blathers on about all this patriarchy stuff as if she had a personal gripe with Moses."

"Why on earth would she bug you, of all people? She must surely know you still have a few arrows in your quiver for a good-looking gent."

"Don't interrupt, Davey, there's a dear. Now this woman—she once did a documentary on divorce for me at the CBC in Toronto—I have a hunch knows our Mr. Zed."

I was so astonished by that remark I couldn't have interrupted if I'd tried, though I dearly wanted to know the genesis of this startling bit of Artemis' intuition. I needn't have bothered, as she followed right on with it.

"She's always yakking on and on about this simply dreadful man she used to know. At one time or other she's told me he has raped his mother, married his sister, and beaten her up and then hung her by her wrists from an apple tree in the backyard until she screamed for mercy. And just for a change of pace he'd stick an electric prod up her thingummy during one of their innumerable rows.

"I'm told all this, ad nauseam, just to show what a misogynist, bully, rapist, and all-round pervert he is. Oh yes, she mentioned that nowadays he also has a boyfriend. Sort of hints that he's done that just because it has become fashionable."

"And you don't believe her?"

"I'll tell you what I believe, Davey. I believe the guy she rants and raves about is her husband AND her brother! She knows just too much about him as a kid—and talks about his parents as if they were hers, too. I also think it could well be your friend at Banff. After all, she says she hasn't seen him for over ten years. But I also believe she has started reinterpreting him through her horrid new eyes that sees everyone with balls as an embodiment of threats and violence to women."

"Well, if that's Zed, I've never met the guy," I pecked back sharply. "Sure, he talks a lot about his wife, but he gives a rather different interpretation of their stormy marriage. So did one of his young girlfriends Troy introduced me to. For instance she said that he told her his wife was insanely jealous, even of his horses, and was a real bitch about his mistresses over whom he's always been perfectly honest. The girl also confided in me that her own children wouldn't talk with her anymore.

"And that's not the end of it. She fancies herself as a midwife and women's counselor but spends most of her time feeding them with nonsensical crap about men and what a trap marriage is."

"Sounds like my friend. Mind you, Davey, did you know that there are those who see old Artemis as an expert on kids and marital problems? I even wrote a handbook on marriage when I was working for those years for the Corp in London. Only I didn't have the gall to use my real name and wrote under 'Diana Ephesia' instead. Considering I've never married, that was just as well!"

"Did your friend say much about Zed's boyfriend? I mean I'm curious how she came to know about Troy, considering she hadn't seen or talked to her ex in years."

"Well, darling, we all tend to move in rather restricted circles, don't we? I mean we may live in this city or that, work at this or that, be straight or gay, but provided we are from the same kind of social background (class, sweetheart, to you) and are roughly in the same age bracket—chances are we will always know what those in the circle are up to. Someone, someday, will write, call, or these days even e-mail us and give us the dirt sooner or later, don't you think?"

What I thought was that my friend Artemis fulfilled such a role better than anyone else I could think of. In *our* circle, at least she had transformed the pretentiously designated "information highway" into a serious and vital mode of gossip. To hell with the commercials, to hell with the talk-groups, to hell with the pen pals. I need the Internet to know whether Edna is still shacked up with Edward, Fred with Jim, and whether that pompous fart Murray's pompous dinner turned out to be a regrettable triumph or a splendid disaster.

Even so, electronic treasure though she is, I am careful not to elaborate on my experience with Troy again. Nor does she mention her Bowen Island friend—though that may well be because of her intense irritation with the more extreme forms of feminism. The Internet can have teeth.

THE HORSES

At first I couldn't hear my uncle's voice over the din of the binder behind me and the three horses as I sat perched high on the bony back of Duke. We had done nearly a further turn around the field of wheat we were harvesting before I looked back.

It was early August, high noon, and the Cornish sun was very hot. Duke sweated freely and my bare legs were chafed and sore in spite of the flour sack Uncle Jan had insisted I place beneath my bottom. The carthorse was too broad for a thirteen-year-old boy to properly straddle, and although the gunny bag minimally protected my thighs, it quite failed to do service as saddle or prevent the horse's huge backbone from jarring my spine and making my bum cheeks ache.

My turning around was as much a mute enquiry as to when we were to stop for lunch and relieve my sore back and stinging flesh, as it was to hear what Farmer Jan was shouting.

I was to be disappointed. "They'm slowing down, boy, 'cause they've forgotten you'm bloody well up there! Give 'em a tickle of that withy I cut and let all three buggers know it b'ain't dinnertime yet. You aren't up there like Lady Godiva just to look pretty, you know! I could've used one of the village maids for that!"

I flushed, turned quickly away, and gave Tommy to my left a quick cut with the willow frond. He responded with a start and an angry shaking of the head. Good! He was the only one I hated among the three horses. Once he had tried to bite me as I put corn in his manger while he stood sullenly in the twilight of the stables.

Uncle Jan, who saw it happen, had given the horse a terrible thrashing. But although Tommy bellowed in pain and pranced so violently sparks flashed from his steel horseshoes on the granite floor, I knew he still hated me. His eyes had grown yellowish white in the enormity of his terror but that fear was reserved exclusively for my uncle.

I turned to the other side of me and gave Violet a similar thwack. She almost started to trot. Violet, mother of the steed on which I was somewhat precariously perched, wanted only happiness for everyone and was always the most eager to please. I was quite sure she regarded me as her lovable little master.

With somewhat more difficulty, I brought the withy branch down on the broad rump behind me—and felt Duke quiver as he, too, strained at pulling the noisy old binder more quickly around the half-mile oblong of still standing wheat.

I was certain he hardly felt my puny slap but I was never really convinced the coal black gelding didn't resent obeying my youthful will. The biggest and strongest of my troika was the hardest to read.

I didn't want to turn more fully around to strike him harder because that would have risked catching my uncle's eye again. I knew very well that the caustic "Lady Godiva" reference was generated by taking off my shirt and placing it on the brass horn of Duke's huge collar. Wearing only brief khaki shorts and sandals on bare feet, I was now virtually naked in Uncle's Methodist eyes.

The sensation of exposed flesh and the honeyed tan a week of such harvesting had yielded made me feel good. I was also aware that working down there in the stubble, stacking the bound sheaves the binder threw out, was my sixteen-year-old cousin Jan, and that twice since I had divested myself of the shirt, he had glanced in my direction as I rode proudly by.

I peered into the gently waving phalanx of uncut wheat, striving to see what beleaguered and now terrified wildlife crouched there. I prayed there were animals ready to flee when their cover was so consumed by the voracious binder there was no option but to run the gauntlet of men and dogs and seek the safety of the surrounding hedges. This, for me, was the supreme moment of harvesting.

I dared hope for a fox, even an improvident but swift-gliding weasel. The previous August, in Farmer Trebilcock's low-lying meadows while mounted on Duke, there had been a tantalizing glimpse of an otter before it reached the safety of bulrushes screening the Amble River. I knew there would be plenty of rabbits, and so did the village dogs which had already begun to assemble.

This thrill equalled the satisfaction of securing the attention of Cousin Jan, and sustaining his interest when we lay together on the narrow bed which we routinely shared when I came from school for those wartime summer holidays.

As I dutifully touched their haunches as the horses endlessly encircled the field, buzzards glided so high above us their mews sounded as puny as that of kittens. My daydreams bounced between images of a lithe weasel gliding through stubble covered with scarlet pimpernel and the chest of swarthy Jan as I squeezed my smaller body into the S of his before drifting comfortably into sleep.

Such incongruous reveries ended abruptly when Jan's grouchy father on the binder-seat finally yelled a halt to the labors of all those scattered about the partially harvested field.

Men, women, and children streamed from a dozen directions to congregate in the shade of a clump of tall elms. In seconds a damask tablecloth was laid below the hedge bank, and wicker baskets crammed with either pasties or apples placed strategically along its length.

Grease-stained straw hats were discarded; work-worn hands run through damp and flattened hair. There was the chink of cider jugs against mugs as liquid refreshments were poured; raucous laughter from the village muscle that had been hired to help stack the sheaves into neat little pyramids.

The ubiquitous dogs barked and begged for food while growling at potential competitors. The girls from our village of St. Keverne retorted with pert quips to the lewd comments from the younger men.

I listened to the exchange of news, of deaths and dire accidents, learned in remote moorland village pubs, visited when working other cornfields for other farmers during this labor-hungry harvest season.

Then I turned away to tend the horses; tethering them to the stoutest branches, providing them with buckets of water and seeing their halters enabled them to graze on the lush grass at their massive feet.

As I serviced my charges with food and drink I lunged angrily at the evil-looking horseflies which zeroed into the harness-chinking shade for their own sanguinary meal. I had a keen proprietary sense over my foot-stomping giants.

I was not a tall boy for thirteen and was rather slight. These factors gave impetus to my feelings of power and superiority over my three huge if obeisant animals. I was also aware of being eyed professionally by the cluster of sprawled helpers as they idly watched me work.

I protracted the activity as long as I could before the delicious aroma of stewing beef and potato insisted I turn to the rapidly diminishing piles of pasties which had not yet been stuffed into hungry mouths.

In distinction to these ravenous oafs, I selected one small enough for a refined taste—and then, just as importantly, sought a congenial spot to eat it. My heart quickened when I saw a space at the foot of an oak—a little removed from the elms and the main assembly of harvesters. There, in the cool shade, slumped the recumbent figure of Cousin Jan.

He was talking to Silas Jago, a toothless old man who had brought his dog for the rabbit chasing when the cutting was completed. His whippet's name was Sport but everyone called it Sportstha behind his back because the retired roadworker for the parish lisped.

I waited patiently to get a word in but the old fool kept Jan's attention, persuading him to lay a bet on his stupid dog. And when that was over, instead of answering my question about the village fete which was coming up, Jan turned his back on me and started to talk to Molly Pentreath who everyone knew was both illegitimate and wanton.

I finished the pasty standing up. Without a word of goodbye from Jan (who was too busy making fatuous remarks to Gross Tits from Lanoe Farm), I made my way disconsolately back to the horses.

I killed two horseflies on Violet and plucked a clump of succulent clover leaves for Duke to eat from the palm of my hand. I retied Tommy to a sapling ash at whose base the grass grew longer and patted Duke's white muzzle and by blowing up his nostril made him sneeze and splutter as he always did in response.

Even that failed to lift my spirits. It seemed hours before Uncle yelled at everyone again and it was time to put the horses back in the shafts and for me to remount Duke.

When Jan grinned at me just before the last patch fell to the chattering teeth of the binder's knife, and only humdrum rabbits scattered in all directions, I just scowled in return.

Back at Polengarrow I deliberately avoided him when it was time to wash up and sit down for supper. I had decided I would punish him until it was time to go to bed and only then, under the sheets and in the dark, would I whisper forgiveness.

I took my resolve to remain aloof further than ever before. After supper I volunteered to take the horses from the stable and let them loose in the field called Bullen. This was something Jan usually did each night.

Uncle gave me a funny look but said I could if I was careful to hang up their bridles on the proper pegs in the stable and lead them by rope halters up the steep hill to where they'd graze for the night. I was also to make sure the gate was closed after I'd set them free.

My aunt had the nerve to query whether I was big enough for the task but as usual he squashed her with an oath and ordered her to stop spoiling me at the expense of his son, Jan. I sat there and smirked at my cousin.

Once outside, though, my attitude altered. It had grown dusk while we were at supper. There was also a mist rising about the various outhouses.

Inside the stables I had to strain my eyes to fulfill Uncle Jan's instructions and by the time I emerged, pulling on the tethers of the three horses, stars pricked the night sky where bats piped shrilly. The scent of jasmine from the farmhouse porch hung heavy on the air.

As twelve hooves clattered and slithered noisily on the lane's granite hill past the well, I noticed something else. My daytime steeds had lost their distinguishing color.

There was no longer a fawn Tommy, a sorrel Violet or an ebony Duke. Each great shape was now mysteriously dark. Only the white blaze on the head of each stood out ghostly in the feeble light. Their heads nodded in unison as they lumbered up the slope. Their eyes were coals of fire.

All three gave vent to loud snorts as we climbed the last few yards to the gate of Bullen field. Violet added a soft whinny. They were excited by what was about to happen. A tremor of anxiety went through my body which now felt cold through the thinness of my summer shirt. I shivered.

Up to the moment I had carefully replaced the wreath of binder cord over the gatepost, even if my spirit did begin to fret, I could still find reassurance in familiar things. Inside Bullen, though, all that changed.

The mist swirled in grotesque wraiths up there. The hedge separating the two parts of the turf-clumped field had largely dissolved from the rabbits creating their underground warrens.

Someone had told me "bullen" was a corruption of a Celtic word meaning "harelipped man." As I led my progressively independent charges to where I intended to loose them, I thought I saw a face fashioned in the mist. It possessed an unsmiling mouth which sported an ugly fissure midway along its upper lip. . . .

I realized I was not going to go further. The horses were now far too excited. Apart from even louder snorting and whinnying the rope of the halters grew ever tauter. I was afraid one or other of my charges would tug theirs out of my hand.

I rushed quickly to Tommy and leaping up as he raised his head in alarm I managed to yank the halter over his ears and set him free. Violet was a shade more co-operative. Although still whinnying madly, she did fractionally lower her head. That allowed me two hands for the giant Duke.

When the rope fell away from him he did something which froze me in fear. I thought I would never breathe easily again. He rose on his back legs to an almost vertical position, came down with a smashing thud to the mound of the rabbit warren and then rolled over and over like a gigantic puppy-dog.

Then they all let out enormous farts. There was nothing humorous about it. Only an elemental defiance. The explosion of their cooped-up wind said go away!

By now the three monsters were all rearing up on their haunches to paw at the stars. Their stomachs rumbled like thunder and weird un-equine sounds arose from their throats.

They started to run in mad circles, stopping only to flop with an enormous thud to the ground and roll over and over in crazy glee before clambering noisily up once more and galloping faster than ever as if chasing one another's cropped tails.

Then they were no longer horses. Gone was benign Violet, her secretive son Duke, and testy old Tommy who resented small boys. Instead, there were the three sacred centaurs from Ancient Greece I had discovered last term at school: Philyra and Cronus, and Philyra's son Chiron whom Zeus had sent as a star in the sky.

I scanned the heavens for the Centaurs, knowing I would not find it. How could I, when one or other of those looming shapes in the thickening mist was in fact the tutor of such Hellenic heroes as Asclepius, Jason or Achilles?

And then we were back from the Aegean to the Atlantic, to three transformed carthorses on a Cornish farm. From their thunderous dance of freedom they turned to gentle loving. Arched necks were rubbed by soft muzzles; chafe marks from human bondage were kissed away and the great feathered hooves drummed songs of mutual encouragement to vibrate through the earth.

I moved slowly back towards the lane. Not seeking safety. I was no longer frightened, only anxious to do their will and remove myself from the intimacy of their rites and games.

Cousin Jan was sitting up in bed reading by the light of our oil-lamp when I joined him. For once he initiated conversation, asking if the horses had been put up field and I had remembered to shut the gate.

I merely nodded as I undressed and put on my pajamas. Instead of striving to engage him in gossipy chat as I usually did when we got into bed, I gave him my back as he continued to read. And then I forgot him and slept—caught up in a sea of arcane dreams where horses lived without the benefaction or even knowledge of the human race.

CLASSICAL SOURCES

Faxes, Friendship, and Artemis. Artemis/Diana, goddess daughter of Zeus, and twin of Apollo. She was active in moonlight, and much associated with women, sex, and childbirth.

Maiden Voyage. Kypris was born of the sea-foam that gathered about the severed parts of the God Uranus when he was castrated by his son, Cronus. Known also as Aphrodite, Plato symbolized her cult as witnessing to both intellectual and sensual love.

Cool Cats. Alcibiades, an Athenian politician (450? BC-404 BC), was reputed by Plutarch to own an unusually large and handsome dog with a splendid tail that he had amputated so that the Athenians would discuss *it* rather than gossip maliciously about him.

On the Road to Clallam Bay. Chiron—half-man, half-horse—suffered great pain and, wishing to live no longer, transferred his immortality to the Titan Prometheus. Zeus set him in the sky as the constellation Centaurus.

The Dirty Secrets of Diomedes. Diomedes was a leader in the Trojan War. He is reputed to have wounded Aphrodite and, after learning the password to gain entry, murdered the sleeping Rhesus, King of Thrace, before stealing his horses.

Nowhere is Far Enough. Gaius Gallus, poet and soldier, and friend of both the Emperor Augustus and Virgil. He was appointed First Prefect in Egypt in 30 BC, but was mysteriously recalled in disgrace for an unknown offense four years later. Augustus consequently formally renounced his friendship and Gallus committed suicide.

Long after Hemlock: In 399 BC, Socrates was brought to trial on charges including not believing in the Gods and the corruption of Athenian youth. He never took fees from the young men who believed in him. He was also reputed to be very ugly yet possessing a radiant personality and a character of *total* integrity. He is purported to have unflinchingly accepted the cup of hemlock, which was the accepted means the death sentence was carried out in the Athens of his time.

Questions and Answers: Artemis (or Diana), Goddess of hunting, was associated with fertility in both mankind and the beasts. She was also involved with childbirth and the abrupt death of pregnant women.

Kan and Mac: Canace was the daughter of Aeolus and Enarate. She fell incestuously in love with her brother Macareus, and for this reason was put to death by her father, or, according to some accounts, committed suicide.

Just Call Me "Theresa": Teiresias, in Greek myth, was a blind Theban seer who may have lost his sight by observing serpents coupling and killing one of them with a stick. As a result, he is purported to have changed into a woman—and later, by committing an identical act, to have changed back to a man again. Because of this experience Zeus consulted him on a conundrum: whether a man or woman derives most pleasure from the act of love.

Down on the Ranch: Poseidon was God of earthquakes and the sea, and later associated very much with horses. He was thus "lord of the waters" and "lord of the earth." The Romans identified him with the water-god Neptune.

Fathers and Sons: Cronus, youngest God of the Titans, was hidden as a child from his father, whom he eventually castrated.

The Torch: When Paris, the son of King Priam, was born, his mother was informed by a dream that she would bear a firebrand who would destroy the city of Troy. Paris was raised by shepherds on Mount Ida where he had a favorite bull as a pet.

Scorned Women: Phanokles' poem, *Kaloi,* speaks of the the musician Orpheus being ardently in love with a man, Kalais. This earns the hatred of the Thracian women, who tear his head from his body for introducing homosexuality into the region of Thrace.

Then and Now: Ares was the only son of Zeus and his wife, Hera. Although he was one of the twelve Olympian gods, he was relatively unimportant and played no heroic role. He was something of a troublemaker inclined to treachery and irresponsible conduct. He had a bastard daughter, Harmonia, by the goddess Aphrodite.

The Voyage: Jason sailed on the Argo to recover the Golden Fleece. His father's half-brother, Pelias, had been warned he'd be killed by a relative wearing only one sandal, which he duly was—by Jason. The latter was himself said to have died at Corinth by a falling piece of the vessel Argos which had earlier transported him.

Orville: "The Erinyes' (Furies) best-known roles in Greek myth are their pursuit of the matricides Orestes and Alkmaion . . . we are told they want to drink Orestes' blood and drag him down to the Underworld." —*Timothy Gantz, Early Greek Myth*

"The heroes also ushered in a new kind of love: that between man and man. Heracles and Iolas . . . Orestes and Pylades—all enjoyed what Aeschylus calls 'the sacred communion of thighs.' . . . Their relationships were long lasting—only death could end them—and their love didn't fade merely because the beloved grew hair on his legs or because his skin, hardened by a life of adventure, lost its youthful smoothness." —Roberto Calasso, *The Marriage of Cadmus and Harmony*

Hid on an Island Dressed as a Girl: Achilles was the only son of Peleus, King of Phthia, and the sea-nymph Thetis. He quarreled with Agamemnon but refused to fight with him, and went to live on an island in the Black Sea. He was a passionate man, devoted to his friend

Patroclus. He was aware of the prophecy that his life was to be short, but before his fateful death he hid on the island of Skiers where he dressed as a girl and called Pyrrha. The taunt of the time was "What was the name of Achilles when he hid himself among the girls?"

The Beautiful Barman of Banff. Ganymede was a beautiful youth carried off by an infatuated Zeus to his great palace on the highest point of Mount Olympus to be his barkeeper (wine pourer). Zeus gave Ganymede's father, Tros, King of Troy, a pair of divine horses. Horses and eagles play a significant role in the myth of Zeus and Ganymede, and the religious justification of love between men and boys for the Greeks.

Adieu, Artemis. There are many conflicting stories about Zeus, the supreme god of Classical Greek antiquity. He was straight, yet he was gay. He was cruel yet magnanimous. He was henpecked, but a tyrant misogynist. He was a cannibal of his own child, a vindictive murderer, a rapist, and an unscrupulous warrior. He was a God of human diversity. From all these, take your pick. I have taken mine.

The Horses. Philyra was loved by Cronus. When the latter's wife found them both together, Cronus changed both himself and Philyra into horses. Philyra's child was the centaur Chiron.

(Author's note: I have included this story as an appendage to this collection because, although not strictly part of the Internet sequence, it is not only chronologically the precursor of all my classically-inspired fiction but contains references to many of the characters inspiring the tales appearing in these pages.)

DAVID WATMOUGH was born in London, England in 1926. He is the author of several novels and short-story collections, the most recent of which is *The Time of the Kingfishers* (Arsenal Pulp Press, 1994); other published books include *Thy Mother's Glass* and *The Year of Fears*. He lives in Vancouver.